W9-CCF-495

JAMES, FABULOUS FELINE

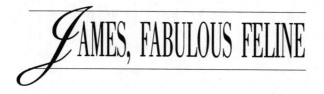

Also by Harriet Hahn

James, the Connoisseur Cat

JAMES, FABULOUS FELINE

Further Adventures of

a Connoisseur Cat

Harriet Hahn

St. Martin's Press   New York

JAMES, FABULOUS FELINE. Copyright © 1993 by Harriet Hahn. Printed in the United States of America. No part of this book may be used or reproduced in any manner whatsoever without written permission except in the case of brief quotations embodied in critical articles or reviews. For information, address St. Martin's Press, 175 Fifth Avenue, New York, N.Y. 10010.

Production Editor: David Stanford Burr
Design by Judith A. Stagnitto

Library of Congress Cataloging-in-Publication Data

Hahn, Harriet.
  James, fabulous feline / Harriet Hahn.
     p. cm.
  ISBN 0-312-09316-0
  1. Cats—Fiction. I. Title.
PS3558.A3235J35 1993
813'.54—dc20   93-692
                  CIP

First edition: June 1993

10 9 8 7 6 5 4 3 2 1

JAMES, FABULOUS FELINE

I had arrived in London the day before with commissions for a number of clients. I am an art expert of sorts and I do research for various individuals and institutions, bid at auction for clients and, on occasion, try to find specific items. This time I planned an extended visit in London.

"Peter in?" I asked Marilyn, who greeted me as I came in. Marilyn's blue-black hair was pulled straight back and worn in a braid on top of her head. She has huge brown eyes, sharp features and a very personal style. She is keenly intelligent and slightly intimidating until you know her. At that moment her handsome face had a tiny smear of white frosting, as she was eating a piece of Penny Black birthday cake.

She grinned at me. "Yes, and hard at work," she said through a mouthful of cake. "Welcome back to London; I'll tell him you are here." She picked up her phone and did so. "Have a piece of cake?"

I shook my head.

"Go right on in," she said. "You know the way."

"You look wonderful," I said, and she did.

I knocked at Peter's door and opened it to be assaulted by a flying grey bomb. I held out my arms and was embraced by a big, silver-grey, short-haired cat with golden eyes, who settled into my arms, grinning and purring.

Peter leaned back in his chair, which not only swings forward and back, but like a barber chair can go up and down as well. Hugging the cat I dropped into one of the wooden chairs. James, for that was the cat's name, wriggled out of my arms, encircled my neck, danced around the back of the chair, jumped to the worktable, where he did two or three somersaults, and then returned to my lap.

"Oh, James, sir," I said. James is an exceptionally aristocratic cat and likes to be properly addressed. "I am glad to see you. And you too, Peter."

Peter also had a piece of birthday cake on his desk because in the Thwaites stamp department this day was being celebrated. It was May 6. A banner printed out on lengths of computer paper was draped across the entry to the third-floor offices. It read HAPPY BIRTHDAY, PENNY BLACK. For those unacquainted with British postal history, the Penny Black was the first adhesive postage stamp and it made its appearance on May 6, 1840.

Thwaites is one of London's great auction houses and Peter Hightower, at seventy-four, is the head and moving spirit of its stamp department. Peter's office sported a big desk, bookcases jammed with books and catalogs, filing cases and a worktable with an excellent light. There were also two very old wooden chairs, comfortable but nondescript, for visitors. Peter himself is of medium height with a ruddy face, white hair, a rounding shape and twinkling blue eyes that miss nothing. He is one of my dearest friends.

There was a knock at the door and Marilyn appeared carrying a tray with coffee for Peter and myself and a saucer of cream for James, who has tasted coffee but doesn't really like it.

"Welcome to London," said Peter warmly. "What brings you to town this year?"

"Two rather dull pieces of research for academics who need to publish and don't want to do all the work. And there is an interesting commission which, if I can bring it off, or if it is there to be brought off, will mean a very handsome fee indeed."

"Let's hear about the interesting one," said Peter.

"It seems there was a French sculptor who made a name for himself in England about 1748. He was not only a very skillful artist but had a great flair for the dramatic, and he executed some marble monuments, particularly funeral pieces, which are still of interest. All I can find out about him at the moment indicates that he was born, or at least baptized, in Lyon in 1702 and then appeared in England in the 1740s. He is known at least once to have made a terra-cotta model of one of his sculptures before he committed it in marble. That one was of Shakespeare, but there is the vaguest hint that he may have made others."

"Yes, yes," said Peter, who not only knows postal history but has a wide-ranging interest in all the arts. "I think I know whom you mean. His name is Louis-François Roubiliac."

"That's the one. If I can find one or more of these terra-cotta models for his statues, presuming he made more than one, and can buy one or more, I stand to make a very handsome fee. My client is a collector of sculpture who has a passion for these dramatic pieces, and I should dearly love to find one. If I do, it will be sheer luck, I think, but I'm going to try."

Peter swivelled around in his chair and searched in a stack of monographs on the floor beside him. At last he found what he wanted.

"Here's old L-F.," he said. "According to this, it is possible that the young sculptor might have gone to Dresden from Lyon. There is the suggestion that he had an uncle in Dresden, an accountant. There was also a fine sculptor working in Dresden in the 1720s when your boy would have been in his teens." Peter began to chuckle. "It so happens we have just taken in a large correspondence covering the period from 1715 to 1738 in Dresden. It is largely commercial and I am starting to look it over just now. I'll see if anything at all suggestive turns up."

James, who had given up the cream and was playing with a wad of paper on the worktable, looked up at me and shook his head.

"You think it's hopeless, do you?" I asked.

James nodded and went on playing.

I got up. "I'm off for now," I said. "You've got a table full of work here and I've got to look in at the Victorian paintings coming up for sale soon. Come by Baron's Chambers about five for a sip or two of the water-of-life, as the Scotch would say."

"Love to," said Peter.

"Want to come with me?" I asked James. He likes to wander in the great room of Thwaites and sometimes sees something he fancies. He is beginning to develop as a collector. He owns three pieces: a Staffordshire porcelain cat, a copy of the Egyptian cat Bastet who wears gold earrings, and a pair of his own gold earrings for which he had his ears pierced some time ago.

This time James shook his head. Then he waved his paw at a

line of bluish stamps on one edge of the worktable. James has extremely acute vision and can detect tiny differences between the printing on different stamps in a much shorter time than can the normal human being. He spends part of his week working with Peter or with Marilyn, sorting for forgeries, reentries and plate flaws. In this case he would look at the stamps lined up for him and very gently move the forgeries out of line with his paw.

James lives around the corner at Baron's Chambers, a building containing small furnished apartments that can be rented for as short a time as a week. He ostensibly belongs to Mrs. March, who manages the building from her apartment on the fifth floor, but he really belongs to the world. When I am in London I stay at Baron's. When James is not working for Peter Hightower, he sits on a small table at the entrance to Baron's and subjects possible tenants to careful scrutiny.

"I'm on the fourth floor in flat twelve," I said to James and Peter as I left. "Come anytime after four."

James gave me his I-know-where-you-are look and then relented and winked and grinned, and I knew my old friend was ready for any adventures we could find.

By four in the afternoon I was back in flat twelve, which has a charming sitting room with a big overstuffed sofa and one overstuffed chair, a glass-topped table that seats four easily and six in a pinch, and six straight chairs in case there *is* a pinch. There is a comfortable bedroom, a bath, and a tiny kitchen now stocked with bottles of Laphroaig single-malt whiskey, La Iña sherry, Strasbourg goose liver pâté from Fortnum and Mason's just down the street, Stilton cheese from Paxton's up Jermyn Street.

I had just settled down in the easy chair when I heard a scratch at the door. There was James. He gave me a nod, walked purposefully into the bedroom and patted my suitcases in approval. James likes tweed suitcases bound in leather—none of your plastic stuff for him. After assuring himself all was well in the bedroom he hurried into the kitchen, where he began opening the cupboard doors. He is good at this. He has had lots of practice. He patted the can of pâté and grinned at the Laphroaig.

"Very good choice," I said. I opened the pâté, put out some crackers, set out two glasses and a saucer and the food on a tray, and at that moment the downstairs bell rang. It was Peter. James and I stood in the hall, watching the tiny elevator rise in its elaborate gilded exterior cage in the center of the stairwell. The lift itself is made of mahogany with windows of bevelled glass cut in it. It moves slowly but with certainty and can hold four moderate-size people with only a little discomfort.

James greeted Peter ebulliently and led him to the sitting room, where Peter settled comfortably in the easy chair. I followed with the pâté and crackers.

"Laphroaig or La Iña?" I asked.

"I'll have La Iña, please," said Peter. He is especially fond of good, dry sherry.

I did not have to ask James. I went back to the kitchen for a glass of sherry for Peter, a glass of Laphroaig for me and a saucer of the same for James. I put the saucer on the coffee table. James sat next to the saucer, scattered a few drops on the table as a libation and lapped, while Peter and I clinked glasses.

We three friends sat for a moment in silence, relishing the delight of being together again after a long separation.

Then my telephone rang.

"Helena," I cried, delighted to hear her voice.

James was galvanized. He nearly knocked the phone out of

my hand as he meowed into it. At the other end I could hear Helena making kissing noises while James purred his loudest.

Helena, Lady Haverstock, a tall, beautiful woman, about thirty, with golden hair and laughing blue eyes, is the wife of Henry Stepton, the 24th earl of Haverstock. Both Lord Henry and Helena are intimate friends of James's. In fact, it was James who brought them together when Helena was a struggling artist in London and Lord Henry a lonely widower. Lord Henry and Helena are also close friends of mine. Helena was calling to welcome me to England and invite James, Peter and myself for the weekend at Haverstock Hall, their estate, which was about an hour's drive from London. I relayed the message to Peter, who thought it a wonderful idea. James was lying on his back and patting his paws together with delight at the prospect.

"We'd all love to come," I told Helena.

"Fine," she said. "Weatherby will be in London Friday with the station wagon and he will pick you three up at Baron's about four if that is convenient."

"That will be super," I said. "We all send love."

I hung up the phone and considered. That left the following day in which to get started on my project.

"James," I said. He was back on the coffee table eating pâté. He always leaves the crackers. "How would you like to come to Westminster Abbey with me tomorrow?"

James looked at Peter.

"Go ahead," said Peter. "I have to spend time on the German correspondence and Marilyn is calling an auction so there is no work for you."

James turned to me and nodded. He loves expeditions around London.

A little later the three of us went around the corner and down the street to Colombino's Restaurant, where James is welcome. Peter and I had cannelloni and salad while James had a dish of clam sauce. James does not like pasta. The three of us split a bottle of good red wine. Outside the restaurant James and I said good night to Peter and walked back to flat twelve in time to watch the late evening news. As we sat before the TV there was a knock at the door. I opened it to find Mrs. March, the charming manager of Baron's Chambers.

"Is James here by any chance?" she asked.

I was about to call, but James was too fast for me. He had streaked out the door and was standing on the stairs leading up to the fifth floor. He somehow gave the impression that he had come to get Mrs. March rather than the other way around.

"He seems to be right there," I said, laughing.

"Silly cat," she said affectionately. "I hope he wasn't bothering you."

"Indeed not," I said. "In fact I should like to borrow him for the weekend. He has been invited to go with me to Haverstock Hall, if you agree."

"Of course he may go if you are sure he won't be any trouble."

I heard James snort. The descendant of the favorite cat of the Stuart kings, the boon companion of the earl of Haverstock be any trouble? Ridiculous!

The next morning when I opened my door to get the *Telegraph*, there was James sitting on the paper and in his mouth was his carry-bag. Last year Lord Henry commissioned Asprey's, one of London's finer shops, to make a bag specifically designed to allow James to travel on the underground, or go to Fortnum and Mason to pick out delicious items for the larder. The bag was made of parachute nylon with a sturdy leather bottom. Around the base of the bag, convenient to a paw, is a series of leather-bound holes, which permit James to reach out. Around the top of the bag is another set of holes at the right height to permit James to look out in all directions. The bag has a flap to cover the top and longish handles so it can be carried over my shoulder. James has taken many trips in it. It has his initial on it in gothic script.

I held the bag upright, James hopped in and I closed the top. He waggled a bit to get settled and we were off to the Green Park station. We changed trains at Victoria and finally arrived at the Westminster stop, walked up to street level and on to the Abbey. James loves to travel on the underground. Occasionally he has been known to scratch a pickpocket he caught in the act, but generally he remains invisible. However, I have to be careful to carry him at shoulder level. If I forget and rest the carry-bag on the floor, James will scratch me, or any leg he can reach.

It was a grey, misty May 7, not quite drizzling, but cold. It was a day to discourage tourists and the Abbey was not overrun with crowds. In a building like the Abbey, James can run free. He disappears in the shadows as soon as I let him out of the carry-bag and I cannot see him. He can, however, see me, so he follows where I am going, at the same time making little forays of his own.

Westminster Abbey is a place of worship and also a shrine to many of the heroes of the nation. Writers, artists, statesmen, military leaders and important clergymen are buried here, as well as kings and queens. For some of the great a simple plaque on the wall is sufficient, but for others great monuments, including many carved figures in marble, have been erected. The Abbey is a vast place and even these monuments are dwarfed in the gloom. I wandered happily, letting my imagination follow where time took me, past sixteenth- and seventeenth-century tombs but always looking for a mid-eighteenth-century monument designed by L-F. Roubiliac, which I knew was there.

I turned a corner and came upon a school group consisting of about fifteen ten-year-old children and a teacher. The teacher was standing facing the children in front of a large monument that consisted of a dying General Wolfe leaning on the arm of an aide and looking off into the infinite. Below him with expressions of grief and gratitude huddled a crowd of men and women wearing the dress of the Puritans, and two or three American Indians with feathers in their hair, also looking gloomy. The monument had been given about 1745 by the Commonwealth of Massachusetts to honor the British general who saved the colony from the French. The monument was very dirty and it was not easy to distinguish details in the dim light.

I stopped to watch because the children seemed so interested.

"This memorial piece," the teacher was saying in a droning voice, "has representatives of all the various people in the colony at the time."

I heard a small snuffly sneeze.

"There it is again," said a boy in the front row.

"Where?" asked his neighbor.

"Just there, on that Indian or whatever he is."

"What is it?" asked another.

"Look, that Indian's feather moved."

I looked too and sure enough, above the tip of a dirty grey marble feather waved for just a moment a grey fur plume.

The teacher, sensing he had lost his audience, changed his direction. "Who can tell me where Massachusetts is?" he asked.

"Look, there it goes again," said one boy.

"I wonder how they do it?" said another.

The plume was waving quite excitedly now and little puffs of dust were rising in the air.

"Batteries, stupid," said a boy from the back of the group.

"Doesn't anyone know where Massachusetts is?" asked the teacher.

"Look," said the first boy, pointing. "It's getting bigger."

"What is getting bigger?" asked the teacher.

"The feather," said the boy. "Just there."

The teacher turned around at last and looked at the monument.

"Aw, it's gone," said one of the boys.

"If we stand still and wait, maybe it will come back," said another.

"You see, there was this extra feather waving back and forth over that Indian's head," a small boy in front explained to the teacher, "but it's gone now."

"He's right," said four or five others together.

"We will move on," said the teacher firmly, and herded his

charges down another aisle with some difficulty as boys kept turning back to see if the moving feather would reappear.

"James," I said when they were out of earshot, "that was a childish trick."

From behind the Indian's feather a grey tail twirled in the air, and I heard a muffled meow.

"Come on," I said with a laugh. "We're almost there. We're looking for the tomb of Colonel Hargrave, done about the same time as this piece but quite different."

James appeared on the aisle and walked beside me, rubbing my leg occasionally, and together we shortly came upon a most unusual monument. Here was Colonel Hargrave. Unlike almost every other hero and heroine who are buried here, whose tombs feature weeping angels or mourning relatives, the marble colonel was leaping out of his grave with an exultant grin on his face. One arm was raised over his head, pulling aside his shroud, and one leg was protruding from his coffin. Here was the colonel resurrected. James and I stood and stared. Then James disappeared. The monument, in once-white marble, was beautifully executed by a very skillful artist.

As I watched, puffs of dust rose from the back of the statue and shortly a grey cat appeared, lying on the marble drapery of the shroud which the colonel's arm was pushing away. He waved a paw at me. I waved back.

"Look it over very carefully," I said. "I will try to take a picture, but the light is terrible here and a flash will make odd shadows."

James appeared and disappeared, dust puffs rose in the damp air and from time to time a pair of golden eyes gleamed at me. I took some pictures and made notes in my notebook. I wondered if there might be a terra-cotta model of this exuberant vision of the resurrection.

James was sitting on the colonel's shoulder gently patting his naked marble chest when I heard footsteps behind me.

"I've had enough," I said in a loud voice apparently to the air as James slipped up beside me and we left the Abbey.

On the way back I dropped off the film I had taken to be developed, and James and I parted company until the afternoon when Peter Hightower came by, suitcase in hand. At four o'clock a station wagon drew up at the entrance to Baron's and we waved from our window at Weatherby, the Haverstock chauffeur, a rangy man who drives with great skill, has great personal dignity and only barely tolerates James, because James tries to show him how to drive by putting a paw on his arm when the speed of the car is not to his liking. However, once we were all on our way, Peter in the back and James and I in the front, James curled up in my lap and went to sleep.

Haverstock Hall, the seat of the earls of Haverstock since sometime in the sixteenth century, is surrounded by extensive grounds, some parts of which have been left wild. It is next to the village of Haverstock, a pleasant place with one small hotel, shops, a post office and a small but choice old church where Helena and Lord Henry were married a little over a year ago. The Hall itself has been added to and subtracted from and rearranged to suit the fantasies of each particular earl in turn since the original building was started in 1543. It is approached by car up a drive of about a quarter of a mile from the main road, and as we came up this drive, I woke James. He peered out the window as Weatherby made a flourishing stop in front of the broad stone steps that led to the massive front door, which was open. There to greet us with open arms was Lord Henry Haverstock, a short greying man of about fifty-five, with a stocky, vigorous body and lively grey eyes. He was dressed as usual in an old tweed jacket and a pair of baggy pants. Beside him was Helena, who is an accomplished artist. Today, as usual, she was wearing a grey smock and white duck pants. At this time in their lives, Lord Henry and Helena were particularly happy with each other and the world, and they radiated this happiness to all their friends.

James jumped out of the car as soon as I opened the door and streaked to Helena's open arms. While James regards Lord Henry as his peer and friend, he is totally in love with Helena. She cuddled him happily, greeted us all and we were ushered into the house while Wilson, the Haverstock butler, supervised our bags and Weatherby took the car away.

Lord Henry, Helena, Peter and I repaired to the library, the favorite room in the house. It is not too big, it has a just-right fireplace, French doors onto a terrace, plenty of bookshelves and big, leather-covered furniture. Lord Henry has his desk here. Helena has a drawing table across the room from the desk. All the mementos that are particularly important to Lord Henry and Helena have found their way here. Over the fireplace is a portrait drawing of James, which Lord Henry bought at Helena's first important show. There are books and magazines around and an air of comfort and contentment. The house has a great many other public rooms. There is the main drawing room, which once held uncomfortably formal French antique furniture. This furniture, much loved by Lord Henry's older sister, Etheria, is now in her castle in Scotland. It has been replaced by somewhat more comfortable and less formal furnishings, but the room is still vast and is used only for large receptions. The state dining room is also used only on special occasions, and a much smaller room, which at one time was a morning room, has been turned into the family dining room, as it is near the kitchen and pantries. There are numerous bedrooms, small sitting rooms, nurseries, and even attics. There is also a great hall at the entrance with a grand stairway curving up to the second floor.

James had left us once we were in the hall because he loves the house, and each time we come he rushes off on a tour of the premises to see what changes have been made since his last visit.

So the four of us sat happily in the library, glad of a fire, even in May. Wilson appeared with a tray on which were all our favorite tipples. Behind him came a footman pushing a trolley with various concoctions Cook thought might tempt us before dinner. A saucer was provided for James, who joined us shortly. He curled up next to Helena and grinned at her.

It was time to catch up.

"Well," Peter chuckled, looking happily at Helena. "When is the big event?"

James looked puzzled. Helena and Lord Henry laughed together.

"So you noticed," said Lord Henry. "I thought the smock covered her pretty well."

"So did I," said Helena, laughing. "I've got about four months to go, and I didn't think I showed that much."

"You look wonderful," said Peter. "But I've been around a bit and I have learned to recognize that really special glow."

James was now really frustrated. He turned from Helena to Peter and at last he patted Helena's arm sharply.

"Sorry, James dear," she said. "I see you don't understand. Henry and I are going to have a baby. That is, I am going to have the baby and Henry is its father."

James still looked puzzled. Helena took his front paw and held it against her abdomen. Suddenly he jerked away and looked intently at a spot on her smock.

"You felt it, did you?"

James looked more and more suspicious.

"Here," she said, and picked him up and laid him on her abdomen. He was tense. He moved uneasily. He made little movements as though he were adjusting to uneven ground. Every once in a while he would jump a little.

Helena held him firmly. "What you are feeling is the next heir to the earldom squirming around inside me. The baby will keep growing until it is big enough and then it will be born and we will all see it and love it. Till then, I am its custodian."

Helena released James. He slid off her and onto the sofa next to her. He shrugged his shoulders. Then he shook his head. Clearly he thought this was a most inefficient system. He snuggled next to Helena and gave her abdomen a furtive glance from time to time.

Meanwhile, we had gone on to hear about Helena and Lord Henry's trip to Gibraltar and their return to Haverstock Hall, where Helena had made many changes, all of them designed to make the Hall a warm and welcoming place. She had happily turned the day-to-day management over to Wilson, who was as delighted in his new mistress as she was in him. Wilson has been the butler at the Hall for at least twenty years. He has been devoted to Lord Henry since the beginning, and it was with the greatest pleasure that he saw Etheria replaced by Helena. Wilson supervises the footmen and maids, who do the work of the house. Wilson is short and round. He can be a sympathetic friend and a demanding supervisor. He regards James as one of the privileged class, but I notice that James never teases Wilson. In the kitchen Cook reigns and a wonderful cook she is. She and Helena plan the meals. Helena often likes to do the marketing as it takes her to the village, where she has been warmly welcomed by tradespeople, clergy and gentry alike. In the west wing of the Hall, Helena has set up a studio where she works at her painting nearly every day. Lord Henry has a keen interest in history and has begun to write monographs. He and Peter share an interest in the details of life and commerce in the eighteenth century.

Peter recounted his travels, which were many and varied. I reported on my search for a perhaps nonexistent statuette.

"I'll bet you find it," said Helena. "I'll bet you a pound you find one before the heir arrives." James had been listening. He tapped her on the arm and shook his head. "Not enough?" she said. James nodded. "Two pounds?" James shook his head and gestured higher. "A Helena Haakon painting?" James nodded.

"Done," she said, and laughed.

"Now I'll have to get it," I said.

"Enough of this delightful conversation," said our hostess. "I want to get to the real reason I asked you down for the weekend. I want you to make up a team with us to play in the Great Croquet Tournament, which will take place at Castle Falling next weekend."

"I think I've heard of it, now you mention it," said Peter. "Viscount Wilter gives it every year just before he opens the grounds of the castle to the public."

"That's it," said Lord Henry. "Quite a lot of people participate and a great many people come to watch. The first prize is the honor of having your name engraved on one of the more elaborate trophies of the world, but the fun is in the game. I used to love it when I was young, but then when Etheria lived here she would not hear of our mingling with riffraff, as she called some of the players, and even though the viscountess was one of her best friends, Etheria flatly refused to have anyone from the Hall play in the tournament."

James's eyes looked cold. James is Etheria's declared enemy and he is not fond of the viscountess.

"Glorious," said Peter. "I love croquet, and it is one of the few games I can play at my age. By all means let's enter."

James looked puzzled.

"Don't worry," said Helena. "We'll have a practice tomorrow morning and you will see it is an interesting game." She stroked James lovingly.

Wilson announced dinner. We spent a happy evening. At last James and I went up to our room.

I lay in bed, ready to turn out the light. James was pacing around. At last he jumped on the bed and put a tentative paw on my stomach and looked at me inquiringly.

"No, James," I said, laughing. "There is no baby inside me." James grinned and jumped on my belly. Then he rolled up next to my ear and purred us both to sleep.

The next morning was a May morning to dream of. The sun sparkled, the air was soft and little breezes danced about. After breakfast the house party, Lord Henry, Helena, Peter, James and I, decided to walk to the village to mail the accumulated letters and see who was out and about.

As we walked down the principal street, stopped in the post office, greeted the postmistress and mailed out letters, Lord Henry and Helena met a number of people they knew. Then we stopped at the village green to greet the Honorable Fiona Wettin, who was there admiring the blossoming apple trees.

An austere woman of middle age, Fiona has the misfortune to be descended from some notable aristocrats. However, she has a very meager income to support her pretensions. At one time she and Etheria were very close friends and Fiona spent many a happy hour discussing the shortcomings of the village residents with Etheria. When Helena first came to Haverstock Hall as a guest, Fiona snubbed her coldly, following Etheria's lead. However, to Fiona's surprise, Helena married Lord Henry and became Lady Haverstock, and Etheria married the duke of Inverness and moved to his castle in Scotland. The Honorable Fiona was now in a delicate position.

"Good morning, Fiona," called Helena.

James, who had been pretending to climb a tree, jumping at it and then falling back, stopped and turned to glare. James does not like Fiona.

Fiona blushed. She bobbed her tall frame up and down in what might be called an attempt at a curtsy and then stopped herself. "Good morning, Lady Haverstock," she said uneasily.

"We are all on our way to the Buttery for morning coffee. Won't you join us?" Helena called.

"Why, thank you," said Fiona, striding up to join us. James glowered.

The Buttery is the village tearoom. We entered, and the six of us settled in at a table. Peter Hightower was introduced to Fiona, and James and I were acknowledged this time with a smile. We had met Fiona before. I smiled, James did not. Fiona greeted me with some warmth. After all, I am from another country. She gave James a look of deep suspicion.

"Does that cat go everywhere with you?" she asked me as a small carton was placed on a chair so James could reach the table. He sat on his box and viewed us all with great dignity.

"He's one of my very best friends," said Helena with a smile. "And he is always invited."

Coffee was served and delicious cinnamon buns. James had a saucer of cream. By chance he was sitting with Helena on one side and Fiona on the other. I could not help but notice that James, who is usually the most fastidious of cats, was slurping the cream, and little drops were flying in Fiona's direction.

"You aren't entering the Great Croquet Tournament, are you?" asked Fiona, clearly expecting that the answer would be no.

"Indeed we are," said Lord Henry. "Our team of four and our coach are right at this very table."

"Well," said Fiona, somewhat taken aback, "wait till Etheria hears this. We are entering, you know. The viscountess, Etheria, the Honorable Lucy Poole and I are a team. I have designed our uniforms." She paused for a minute. "Who is your coach?" she asked.

"James," said Lord Henry, looking very serious.

James looked up, startled. He had no idea what a coach was.

Fiona laughed, a full, happy, exultant laugh. "I wish you all the luck in the world," she said. I felt she thought us no competition at all.

With that she stood up, picked up her handbag, brushed the tiny drops of cream off her tweed skirt and smiled graciously on us all. "Thank you for the delicious coffee," she said, "and I look forward to seeing you on the playing fields of Castle Falling." We all smiled. She turned to go, managing to bash James on the head with her handbag as she did so.

"Look here," said Lord Henry, turning to Helena, "you certainly need not be pleasant to that woman. She certainly was unpleasant enough to you when you first came here."

Helena reached over and patted Lord Henry's hand. "I know that Etheria was not interested in mingling with the people in the village, but I love the village and all its inhabitants. I don't want enemies and factions, so let's make friends with Fiona. We won't have her to dinner every night, but I think we might be pleasant."

James was giving Helena his you-are-truly-odd look.

"I don't ask you to like her," she said to James, "but really it costs me nothing and it is funny seeing her struggle with my new status."

"Come on," said Peter Hightower, who had paid the bill and was growing anxious to leave, "we must get back to the Hall for a practice session. I'd like to beat that woman."

In our absence, Wilson had set out a croquet court on the lawn beyond the terrace outside the library. After lunch we trooped outside to practice.

"James," I said, "the object of this game is to hit the big wooden ball with this mallet through the hoops called wickets in the proper order and finally to hit this wooden stake. The first player to complete the course successfully wins the game. There are a lot of rules governing which player may hit another's ball and when but we'll find those out as we go along."

He watched me as I shot a practice round. Then he got my attention, pointed to the stake at the end of the court. I placed my ball some distance away and aimed the mallet. James placed himself behind the stake and gestured with his tail to the left. I corrected the aim. He flicked a bit to the right. I had clearly gone too far. I made a correction. He nodded. I hit the ball, right on the mark but too hard. We tried again. I read the signals for direction and then, by flicking his tail back and forth, James gave me an approximation of the amount of force required. It worked. I hit the stake with just the right amount of impact.

The rest of the team assembled, and James and I showed them our system. There followed a period of intensive practice. Our most accurate player was clearly Helena. Before long she was reading the right speed and direction of the ball almost as well as James himself. Lord Henry and I were about on a par, while Peter had some problems because he is a little tubby. However, once we began to play, it became evident that Peter was by far the shrewdest strategist.

The weather held and except for attendance at church services Sunday morning, where James behaved to my surprise with great dignity until after the service, when he rode on my shoulder and waved to the congregation and patted the vicar on the head, we practiced croquet. We thought we were getting very good indeed.

James had made one significant discovery. The croquet ball was too large for him to move by pushing it with his front paws, but if he ran at it, he could move it, and if he leaned his haunch against it, he could displace the ball a short distance. However, playing with a croquet ball bored him. He preferred acting as our coach.

We returned to London Sunday night. Weatherby dropped James and me off at Baron's. It had turned cool again and I made some hot chocolate, which James has taken a liking to, and we sat on the sofa to watch the late news.

"You are a great coach," I said, stroking the sleek grey back.

James nodded. He knows how good he is but he does enjoy having someone else tell him.

There was a knock. It was Mrs. March.

"I hope James was not a nuisance this weekend," she said.

James had slipped out the door and was lying on the stairs flicking his tail from side to side. I pretended to aim a mallet. Then he waved his tail back and forth with a great flourish. I pretended to swing a mighty swing and James himself raced upstairs.

"He was a great asset," I said.

"That's nice," said Mrs. March, and followed James.

The following week was short as we were to go to Haverstock Hall Thursday evening to get ready for the tournament, which would start on Friday. We went to Harrods on Monday and purchased a mallet and two croquet balls. I made a wicket out of cardboard. Thereafter I was able to practice on the rug with James's coaching. He also practiced leaning against the ball to move it slightly but that proved ineffective, so he practiced flinging his whole body at it after a brief run and that method moved the ball quite well.

Peter Hightower came by Monday night and we discussed strategy. James came to understand that not only do you try to get your ball through all the wickets in sequence, but you actively try to prevent your opponent from doing the same by knocking him away from his intended wicket. James also became gradually familiar with the complicated system of "turns." One extra turn for going through a wicket, two extra turns for hitting another ball unless you had hit it before and had not gone through a wicket, all accumulated turns wiped out when going through a wicket except the one for going through a wicket, etc. As Peter and I discussed these, James shook his head as though bothered by a swarm of gnats.

"Don't worry about all this," said Peter, taking pity on James's confusion. "I understand it and so do the referees. Your job is to keep our aims accurate and our speeds appropriate, and my job will be to figure out the best use of our shots."

James nodded his relief and retired to the windowsill where

he loves to watch what is happening on Ryder Street, if nothing more exciting is at hand.

James did have something more on his mind, though, and Tuesday he insisted we go out. He refused to travel in the bag. He was leading this expedition. I followed along as he led me to a street market. Once at the market he demanded to be carried so he could see the tables, and finally he found what he wanted. A table selling large plastic initial pins. James indicated a J pin in a deep shade of royal purple. I asked how many he wanted, because I wasn't sure what he had in mind. He nodded his head five times so I bought five pins. We were not through. Close by was a table selling white baseball caps. James was delighted. He jumped up and down in my arms. I tried one on. It fit. I bought four. The salesman directed me to a stall not far away where I found a doll's white hat for James. We took our purchases back to the flat and I pinned the Js on the caps. James had gotten us our team identity.

Lord Henry and Helena dropped in Wednesday for a chat, as Helena had been in London to see her doctor. Lord Henry now knew how the tournament was to be arranged. There were to be three classes. Singles, doubles and team of four. Friday the first round of singles would start at nine A.M. and the first round of doubles would take place in the afternoon.

Saturday would see the first round of team of four and the second round of singles. Then lunch, the second round of doubles and the second round of team of four. Sunday would be a really hectic day. There would be three semifinal rounds in the morning and three final rounds in the afternoon. Sunday evening all sixteen teams, the referees and marshals, and the families of the participants would all assemble for the awards banquet and celebration.

Helena was delighted with our hats. She took James's hat with her. "I'll attach some strings so you can keep it on," she said.

"Can you be ready at the usual time tomorrow, say about four o'clock?" asked Lord Henry as he and Helena were leaving. "Weatherby will come by and pick you up as he did last week."

"Fine," I said, and James nodded excitedly.

After they had gone, we practiced awhile on the rug and then we went into the kitchen to see what the larder had for us to eat for dinner. It was raining as usual and we didn't want to go out, so we settled for a smoked salmon sandwich and a bottle of stout shared between us.

I noticed that James was practicing a winner's stride as he left that night and walked upstairs even before Mrs. Marsh came to call.

We drove with Weatherby Thursday afternoon as arranged and on Friday morning, in the sun, with very little breeze, we drove off early for Castle Falling and the tournament.

Castle Falling is one of the oldest castles in England. It was originally a fortified stronghold and sits on a rise that commands the country around it. The eleventh-century stone castle sits in the center of an oval earthworks. On two sides of the castle the oval opens to provide a flat green large enough to hold two croquet courts. The whole oval is bounded by a steep-sided earth barrier, now covered in grass, that provides seating for the spectators at the tournament. Outside the earthworks is a moat, still full of water and now inhabited by ducks and swans. A bridge crosses the moat and a road leads to the entrance to the castle. Originally a drawbridge, at the present time it is a permanent footbridge. The castle itself is not habitable, but it is one of the more romantic ruins in the area and it is a very popular site for tourists in the summer. The viscount and viscountess live in a charming residence that dates from about 1675 and is always referred to as the "new house." It is a mile or so away from the castle. As we left the main road and wound gently higher toward the castle, which we could see from some distance away, we passed through meadows where sheep graze at some times and cars park at others. On this particular Friday the cars, even that early in the morning, outnumbered the sheep.

Weatherby let us out at the bridge and disappeared with the wagon. A yellow and white striped tent took up a large part of the space to our left. In it were food concessions and stalls where pennants of various colors were sold. We crossed the drawbridge and found another tent labelled PARTICIPATING TEAMS HERE. This tent filled all one side of the road leading to the castle. On the other side a barrier had been erected with a small gate for a ticket taker, who was doing a brisk business.

We registered in the participating teams tent, were given a program and directed to a set of bleachers set up against one wall of the castle. These bleachers, one on each side, were reserved for the contestants and had a splendid view of both courts, the spectators sitting on the earthworks; beyond were the fields and downs and the glorious blue sky without a trace of cloud. I noticed that pets were welcome. Some people had brought dogs and others cats so James was able to sit on the bleachers with us.

We looked around. We all put on our hats. Helena had sewn some strings on James's hat and she tied it on at a fetching angle.

Opening her program and nodding at James, she explained to me, "This is how it works. The teams are all listed in the program and each team has both a number and a color. We are pale green, and our number is 12. Each of us has a number. I am 12–1, Henry is 12–2, Peter is 12–3 and you are 12–4. At one end of each court you will see a flagpole. The pennant flying on the pole is the color and shows the number of the person or persons to play there. Between the two courts you will see three tall poles, now empty. On those poles will go the pennants of the winners of singles on the first, doubles on the middle, and on the last, team of four."

James brushed gnats away and I was not sure whether they were real gnats or just a sign of confusion.

"Don't worry, James," said Helena, "you will see it clearly as the day goes on. Let's see who we know."

We looked over at the competitors' bleachers. Many of the teams were in elaborate costume. There was Fiona Wettin with the viscountess, the Honorable Lucy Poole and Etheria, the duchess of Inverness. They were dressed in doublets and hose with gold crests emblazoned on their doublets. The only member of the team for which the uniform was unfortunate was Etheria, who has very heavy legs. A cousin of the queen had come with a team of her own dressed in tabards with the lion and the unicorn painted on them. Some teams had no special clothing. Our caps were exactly right—not too elaborate, but still indicating we had made a team effort. Since many of the teams knew one another there was much waving and gesturing.

My number was called for singles play early in the morning, and at that time I discovered that only the players and, on occasion, a referee were permitted on the court. However, James could sit on the sidelines and I discovered that he could offer considerable help by signalling with his tail. With his help I successfully defeated a young man in full evening dress wearing a large button that identified THE BUTLERS. Each court had a referee, who retrieved balls hit out of bounds and resolved any disputes during the play.

At the end of the game, my green pennant went up on the singles pole and at the end of the morning, when the first round of singles had been completed on all four courts, all of our green pennants were flying on the winners' pole. We noted that all four orange pennants belonging to the viscountess and her team were also flying on the winners' pole.

There was a break for lunch and we gathered at one end of the stand where a Haverstock footman arrived with a picnic hamper, the contents of which we devoured. We were all very hungry. Lunch over, Helena stretched out and napped while James and I decided to explore the castle. We wandered through the great hall whose ceiling was partly gone, through various rooms toward the back and at last came to the gift shop where dish towels with the castle on them, postcards, souvenirs and plants were available. The shop was in an enclosed room with a small stove. This coal stove was often used on cold June days. Just outside was a coal pile. James sniffed it, discovered the black coal dust, sneezed and stalked away.

We returned to the stand and prepared for the doubles competition. Lord Henry and Helena played as a team on court one, and Peter and I played on the other side of the castle on court four. James raced frantically back and forth trying to support all his dear friends.

Peter and I won our game easily as Peter drew the last position, which in croquet is a great advantage. He finished in a flourish, passing up all the rest of the players, and became a rover, which meant he could interfere with the opposition and assist me by putting himself in my way so I could hit him and earn two more turns. Peter is a master of the strategy of the game. He was occasionally distracted as James did not understand the concept of a rover and sat on the sidelines howling in anger as Peter roved the court. On court four Helena and Lord Henry won handily, so a happy team returned that night to Haverstock Hall. On the way home Peter explained the function of a rover to James, who eventually gave us his I-knew-it-all-the-time look and went to sleep on Helena's lap.

Saturday dawned clear and warm. Insects exulted and the players trooped to the second day, which opened with the first round of team-of-four play. James was beside himself and finally retired under the stands and covered his head with his hands. In fact, there were constant calls to the referee to settle disputes. Balls crashed into each other and at last, when the round was over, sixteen teams had been reduced to eight. Hanging on the winner's pole were our four pennants, those of the viscountess, Etheria, Fiona and the Honorable Lucy. Fiona's deadly aim and Etheria's ability to intimidate the other team had brought them through. Also on the pole were the flags of the Butlers and the Royals, as the team fielded by the queen's cousin was known, as well as four more.

After a fifteen-minute interval the second round of singles was called. I won from Peter, who was delighted to lose. He was ready to sit awhile. Lord Henry played his sister Etheria in an emotional match fought bitterly to the last stroke and won by Lord Henry.

He held out his hand and said, "Good game, Etheria." She stalked away.

In our team, Helena, Lord Henry and I moved up a round.

There was considerable time when I was not playing, and James, once satisfied that Helena had won her match, was bored, so he went exploring the battlements of Castle Falling. James had climbed to the top of a wall and was lying on the stones sunning himself and looking out over the countryside, when out of the sky plummeted an osprey right at James who, taken completely by surprise, rolled off the battlement. I tried to run for him, but there were weeds and stones in the way. I was afraid James might be hurt, but I need not have been concerned. Someone else, an attractive young man with soft, brown hair and darting brown eyes, had caught James as he fell.

"Thanks for saving James," I said as I caught up with the two of them.

The young man, who was dressed in the full-dress clothes of the Butlers, set James gently on the ground. James shook himself and stretched to see nothing was out of place. Then he assumed his elder statesman expression to recover his dignity.

We introduced ourselves. James formally extended a paw. The young man's name was Roger Ham. He did something in the City and had been wiped out of the singles competition by Fiona.

When I told him I was a researcher in the arts he suddenly smiled, and his face, which had seemed almost morose in repose, changed completely, came alive with pleasure. "You wouldn't know what has happened to a splendid painter named Helena Haakon, would you?" he asked eagerly. "I haven't seen her work displayed in any galleries recently."

James grinned his I-know-something-you-don't grin and, patting Roger on the leg to indicate he was to follow, headed off to the stands where he knew he'd find Helena resting. For a moment Roger was confused.

"Follow James," I said. "He will lead you where you want to go."

"Okay," said Roger, and off they went. I followed a little behind and watched as James presented Roger to Helena. I could see Roger introduce himself and sit down beside Helena, and they were shortly in animated conversation. I noted that Roger's eyes were glazed with adoration.

James sat to one side and smirked, but I knew he would not be content to sit for long. Discussions of art bore him.

I need not have worried. Round two of the doubles competition was called at that moment and a young woman member of the Butlers team introduced as Jane Jensen came to collect Roger, who was her partner. At the end of the round Helena and Lord Henry, Peter and I, Roger and Jane, and Etheria and Fiona survived. The only other noteworthy event of the afternoon was the substitution brought in for the Honorable Lucy Poole, who had sprained her ankle while climbing on the castle. The new member of the team was an attractive young woman named Ellen Bruce.

With the doubles finished for the day, the next round of team of four was played, and at its end the Butlers beat us despite the fact that Roger seemed helpless whenever he looked at Helena. Jane was a steely competitor and she and Peter waged a war of the rovers that brought applause from the spectators. The Butlers moved up to play Etheria's team in the semifinals Sunday.

The day's play was over. We walked through the crowd to the drawbridge to look for Weatherby and found Roger and Jane walking beside us.

"Where are you staying?" asked Helena.

"Jane and I are doing bed-and-breakfast in the village of

Haverstock," said Roger. "The others on our team are staying with a local relative. I've got my car here," he added.

"Come by Haverstock Hall as soon as you can for tea or drinks or whatever you'd like and I'll show you my latest paintings, if you'd really like to see them," said Helena.

"Like to? I'd be thrilled," said Roger.

They came shortly after we arrived at the Hall. Roger and Helena retired to her studio. Jane has shiny, straight black hair cut in a severe bob with bangs, which is very becoming to her slightly angular face and thin well-coordinated body. She is a highly organized and intelligent girl with an intense interest in many things. She runs her own public relations firm and she and Peter talked at length about the image problems at Thwaites. James was not greatly interested and spent the time trying to control a golf ball on the carpet.

Eventually, Helena and Roger returned, and he and Jane went off to join their teammates for dinner. We went in to dinner ourselves and then turned in early.

James and I stood at the window of our room and looked out at the half-moon hanging in the sky.

"Do you approve of Roger?" I asked. I like to know how James feels about new people. Sometimes, if he disapproves of someone, he can be difficult.

He nodded his head enthusiastically. Happily we agreed, as I liked Roger myself.

"What about Jane?" I asked.

James purred. He nodded, jumped off the windowsill where he had been sitting and pounced on the bed. I joined him, and we were soon asleep.

The weather held. Sunday was as sunny and warm as the previous two days. A few tiny white clouds lent interest to the sky. We were off for the final day and a certain change had come over James. While we were out of the team of four, Lord Henry and Helena were still alive in the doubles competition and Lord Henry and Helena were both alive in the singles tournament. James was getting interested. There was a chance we might win at least one and maybe two events. He ceased to roam the ruin looking for rodents and settled down on the sidelines to concentrate on the games.

The opening event was the team-of-four third round, where we rooted for the Butlers who were playing Etheria's team. James did his best to distract the new member of the team, Ellen Bruce, who did look marvelous in doublet and hose, but she did not lose her concentration. Also, Roger had lost all interest and kept waving at Helena, so the Butlers lost, but not ignominiously. On another court, the Royals beat a team composed of Victorian ladies in bustles. In team of four the Royals would play Etheria's team in the finals.

The third round of doubles pitted Helena and Lord Henry against Roger and Jane, and it was a match filled with errors. James prowled the sidelines trying to signal either Lord Henry or Helena, but it was hopeless. Roger was so polite to Helena she felt she had to reciprocate. Lord Henry, who was overly protective of the mother-to-be anyway, was distracted, so Jane, moving directly to her goal, won the match for her team. Elsewhere, one pair of Royals was beaten by the other pair of Butlers, and Etheria and Fiona were, to everyone's surprise, beaten soundly by a pair of Victorian ladies who laughed over every shot and so annoyed Etheria that she blew up.

The third round of singles ended with a quarter-final pairing of Helena against a young Royal, Jane against a Victorian lady, a Butler against a Victorian, and Lord Henry against Fiona. The four quarter-final games were played simultaneously on the four courts, and Peter, James and I were kept busy running from court to court. At last the results were in. Helena, Jane, Fiona, and a Butler had survived. Our hopes now lay with Helena.

It was decided that the semifinals would be played at once. Then the contestants would have time for a long lunch and rest, and the finals would be played in the afternoon.

Fiona dispatched her adversary in short order on the court on one side of the castle. On a court on the other side, Helena and Jane faced off. Helena was tired and for a while it looked as though Jane might win. James set himself to be a constantly moving object, always in Jane's sightline. He developed the sharp meow just as she was about to hit the ball and the pounce at an imaginary mouse just as she had lined up her shot, but to no avail as far as we could see until the end of the match. I don't know whether it was a sudden case of overconfidence or the efforts of James, but Jane aimed at the stake, gave a dramatic sweep with her mallet, James yowled, and she missed badly. Helena took the opening provided and won. The finals in the singles competition would be between the Honorable Fiona Wettin and Lady Helena. James was wild with excitement. Lord Henry was worried, and the rest of us rejoiced.

As for the other games, the team-of-four final would be between Etheria's team in doublet and hose and the Royals in tabards, and the doubles finals would see one pair of Butlers play the other.

It promised to be an interesting afternoon. Team of four would play first, doubles second and singles last.

Now that the field had been reduced to the final contestants, the viscount provided a splendid luncheon for the teams participating in the finals in the contestants' tent. He had thoughtfully provided a cot on which Helena could stretch out if she chose, and she did. She was surrounded by not only Lord Henry, Peter and me but Roger Ham and the new member of Etheria's team, Ellen Bruce. James sat next to her and scowled at us all. At last, Helena sent us all away.

Roger and Ellen wandered off together, and James and I went outside to check the court where Helena's match would be played. It was a glorious afternoon, a faint dust scattering the sunlight in the air. The pennants of the players fluttered on the players' poles. Spectators now covered the earthworks and some hung from the ruined windows of the castle.

We wandered through the castle and out past the gift shop. James stopped to examine the coal pile. It was very dusty. On the courts that would not be used we found some young men removing wickets while a group of children played with a pair of Welsh terriers. James watched them carefully. At last he ran out onto the field in sight of the dogs. They immediately gave chase, but they are small dogs with short legs and James easily outdistanced them. He then insisted we return to the courts where the matches were to be played. He found a croquet ball lying on the grass and ran at it as hard as he could, streaking over it but moving it some small distance in the process. Then he seemed satisfied that what he had practiced in the apartment seemed to work and went to sit on the stands to wait for play to begin. I was worried. What did he have in mind?

Trumpeters appeared and blasted on their trumpets. Spectators who were wandering assembled, including the children and their dogs. The contestants for the team-of-four finals were introduced and the game began.

Etheria's team was doomed from the start. Etheria herself was the cause. She is intensely snobbish and when faced with four members of the royal family, if only cousins, she could not restrain the impulse to curtsy and paid no attention to her game. Fiona did her best, but her mind was on the finals. The viscountess was more interested in the arrangements for the awards banquet to follow and kept forgetting it was her turn. Ellen played passably but was clearly interested in catching the eye of an eligible young man. The Royals won. James grinned.

The doubles final between the four members of the Butlers team was a more or less jolly affair. Jane and Roger won in a walk, and then all four hung on one another's shoulders laughing.

Now at last was the moment our team had been waiting for. The trumpeters trumpeted. Helena in her white cap with a big purple J on it and a white billowy, summer dress joined Fiona, in her doublet and hose. The viscount tossed a coin, and Helena called "heads." It came up tails. Fiona chose to go second and the game began.

Both players were very skillful, and the advantage seesawed back and forth. About the middle of the game, James, who had been getting more and more nervous, disappeared entirely.

The spectators were very quiet. The game was nearing its end. Fiona's ball lay in front of the last wicket. A well-directed shot through the wicket would hit the last stake and win the game. Helena's ball was behind Fiona's but also in perfect position. However, it was Fiona's turn to shoot. The game seemed over. Fiona had won. As she approached her ball, there was a sudden disturbance among the spectators. Suddenly a black cat streaked across the field followed by the two Welsh terriers. The cat ran right across the area of play and the dogs followed. The cat disappeared under the stands. The dogs were caught by a referee and returned to the children who were standing on the sidelines.

When play was resumed it appeared that Fiona's ball was no longer in perfect position. Instead it was lying impossibly against the wire of the wicket itself. It would require at least one shot to get back in position, but it would also be in perfect position for Helena to remove it. The game had been turned around.

The referee was called. Fiona demanded that she be allowed to replace her ball. Etheria entered the argument and demanded that Fiona be awarded the game. The referee, perhaps irritated by Etheria's manner, decided that, as had happened on other occasions during the tournament, acts of God and animals were just the breaks of the game and that no relief would be given.

Fiona was angry. She slashed at her ball. It bounced against the wicket and rolled farther away.

Helena approached her ball. She looked over at the stands where, lying on the grass underneath, a cat was grinning at her. Then she took her mallet and, pretending to try to hit Fiona's ball, knocked her own ball away.

Fiona recovered and hit her ball into position again. Helena hit a poor shot from some distance away. Fiona played her final shot and hit the stake. The game was over. The stands erupted. Etheria rushed onto the court and hugged Fiona. Fiona, looking puzzled, brushed Etheria aside and held out her hand to Helena. "That was very sporting, indeed," she said. "You could have won."

"No," said Helena, smiling. "It wouldn't have been fair, but thank you for a splendid game."

Then Helena returned to the stands to join the rest of us.

James climbed out from under where we were sitting and glared at everyone. The trumpets blared and Fiona's pennant was run up the winners' pole.

James, who was covered with coal dust, was glaring at Helena. He batted at her arm and coal dust flew around.

"James, dear," said Helena slowly, "you must not be angry. I appreciate that you wanted me to win, but that is not the way."

James gave her a disgusted look. She should have won. He had fixed it all up.

He looked at the rest of us, to Lord Henry, Peter, Roger, who was sitting with us, and me. We all looked grave. We all shook our heads.

Ellen, who seemed for the moment to have attached herself to Roger, grinned at James. "I thought it was a very clever move," she said in a breathy voice.

"Clever, maybe, but not sporting," said Roger.

"You see," said Helena, "the game has rules and if it is to have any value as a game, you must play it by the rules. If you break the rules to win, there is no sense to the game. I had to give Fiona the game because, before you appeared, she was in a position to win. She might have blown it, but all I did was give her the opportunity to get back to where she was and if I had not done that, I could never have accepted the prize if I had won. It's a matter of sportsmanship."

"Oh," said Ellen.

One of the Royals appeared. "I have to congratulate you," he said. "That was a very sporting thing you did."

Helena smiled. "It was a fine game," she said, "and truly the best woman won."

James looked from one to the other again.

"She's right," said Peter, "there is no point in winning by cheating."

James began to quiver, and coal dust blew all over. Helena picked him up and put him on her lap, coal dust and all. "You are my dearest friend and I love the impulse that made you want to help," she said. "Now let's get clean and go to the banquet."

I had never seen such a change in James. He had been ashamed of himself once when he fell into the baptismal font at the village church during a service, but then he was ashamed because he had been showing off and he knew it. Now he was not only ashamed because all his friends and his peer, Lord Henry, had made it very clear that an action he had carefully planned in order that Helena could win the championship was wrong, was in fact so wrong she had to throw the game away to make up for it.

He kept watching us all through the banquet, which was held on the grounds where only hours before croquet courts had been laid out. The delicious food and wine were brought by caterers in large trucks that also functioned as serving stations.

In the long summer twilight, as candles flickered on the tables in what tiny breeze there was, we toasted one another and laughed, all except James who curled up on the chair provided for him, put his paws over his head and responded to no one. Helena tried to tempt him with food. He simply shook his head. She stroked him gently, ignoring the coal dust that still clung to his grey fur. "I love you, James, sir," she whispered. "I think the feeling behind your gesture was wonderful." James gave a tiny meow, but he refused to participate. His spirit, at least for the moment, was badly bent.

Trophies were handed out at last, and speeches made by the viscount and by the winners. The team of four Royals, represented by a tall, bald fellow, thanked everybody and hoped to play again next year. As he was about to sit down he remembered something. "I want to compliment the directors of the tournament and particularly the players for the high standard of sportsmanship displayed."

The Butlers pair thanked everybody and were appropriately solemn for as long as they were at the podium. They collapsed in laughter as soon as they had made their acceptance speech.

Fiona rose to receive her trophy to the enthusiastic applause of her team. Etheria looked at Helena and gave a little toss of her head that said, "Those of us who are superior will always win."

Fiona had a strange look on her bony face. It seemed to be compounded of fear and confusion. Her normally loud and somewhat grating voice was muffled.

"I'm glad I won the trophy," she said. "It is a source of satisfaction to our team, but I have to acknowledge that not only was my opponent a skillful player, she was also"—there was a short pause—"an uncommonly gracious and sportswomanlike contestant."

A roar of applause went up on the part of everyone except Etheria, who now directed her animosity to Fiona.

"Poor Honorable Wettin," I thought. "Her noble connection, the duchess of Inverness, is about to cut her off. No wonder she looked afraid."

"That took courage, considering the circumstances," I said to Helena.

"Yes," said Helena, "and we must remember that."

At last the time came for the party to break up. Lord Henry, on behalf of the contestants and their families and supporters thanked the viscount and viscountess, and we walked toward the drawbridge and Weatherby. I carried an inert James, though at least his eyes were open. Roger and Jane caught up with us and so did Ellen Bruce. This very pretty girl with long, lovely legs and wavy black hair to her shoulders seemed to have attached herself to us.

Back at the Hall I stood in front of my window looking out at the night. James sat on the windowsill. He was very depressed. I got a brush I carry for him and brushed the last of the coal dust out of his coat. He usually loves brushing, but now he passively let me finish, then he hopped off the windowsill and plopped himself on the foot of the bed.

"Good night," I said as I climbed in.

All I heard in response was a sort of sob.

 **P**erhaps in sympathy with James, the fine weather disappeared, and rain and drizzle with occasional gusts of cold wind descended. On our return on Monday after the tournament, James had dragged himself up to the fifth floor, and there he stayed for two days. At last on Wednesday, he appeared at five in the afternoon, accepted only cream, sat on the windowsill looking out at the rain, and then refused the offer of a dinner at Frank's or Colombino's. Instead, he stalked gloomily back upstairs. Peter asked after him. Mrs. March was worried about him. I was a bit concerned myself, as James had always bounced back before.

Sunday he came early in the morning and insisted we go out. It was a little warmer and showed some signs of sun and I thought he wanted a walk, but he led me directly to St. James's Church, where we listened to a sermon on sin and redemption. James, who had never listened to a sermon before even when he had to sit in the village church at Haverstock, sat perfectly still through it all. Then he wandered around the churchyard for a time and at last headed back to Baron's Chambers.

When we got to my flat, I found a note under my door.

James sat on the stairs while I read it.

"Do you feel well enough to meet people this afternoon?" I asked. "I really need you."

James nodded in a perfunctory way.

"Roger Ham is coming with Helena and some others; that's what the note says."

James laid his head on his paws and looked miserable.

I went into my apartment, and James followed. He jumped on the easy chair, stood on the back of it and looked at himself in the little mirror with the gold frame that hangs just above the chair. He saw a scruffy cat with dull, despairing eyes and unkempt fur.

Soon the bell rang and I admitted Roger and Helena and, to my surprise, Fiona Wettin.

James retreated to the windowsill and looked at us from a long distance. A sinner in jail, not permitted to participate.

"Helena consented to come to town to install the painting I bought from her in my office," said Roger, by way of explanation.

"I think it will do very well on the wall across from your desk," said Helena. "It is nice to have someone pay attention to my work for a change." Then she turned to Fiona. "We met Fiona at the Savoy where we stopped in for coffee and offered her a ride home."

Fiona smiled her funny smile. "I must say it is very good of you, Lady Haverstock, to do this," she said.

"For heaven's sake call me Helena and let's be friends," said Helena.

Fiona blushed. "Thank you, Helena," she said.

I now produced tea and ginger biscuits, and James, after some coaxing, consented to sit next to Helena and let her stroke him gently.

"I'm afraid I have been presumptuous," said Fiona, once we were all provided with refreshment. "I have asked Ellen Bruce to stop in for a few minutes."

James looked up and snarled. I was surprised at the suggestion of an apology in Fiona's announcement. Usually she simply does as she wishes.

"Fine," I said. "As I remember, she's the girl with the big eyes and the stunning legs who was on your team after Lucy sprained her ankle."

"Exactly." Fiona was rapidly returning to form. "She is a very distinguished young person, a direct descendant of Robert the Bruce of Scotland."

We all nodded to indicate we knew how important Robert the Bruce was.

"Etheria found her," Fiona continued, "at a festival in Edinburgh and felt that a girl with her background should not be waiting tables. She seems to have some dramatic talent, so Etheria is paying her tuition at the Royal Academy of Dramatic Art and giving her a small allowance. She lives in London now. I'm not sure a career in the theater is quite the right thing for one of her breeding, but Etheria seems to think it is all right."

"She certainly has the looks for it," said Roger with a sigh.

James hissed at him.

Then the doorbell sounded and Ellen herself made an appearance.

I offered her tea, which she accepted, and a chair, which she declined in favor of sitting on the floor next to Roger, stretching her handsome legs out and resting her back against his chair. She made a most attractive sight.

She didn't so much talk as make little flattering noises every time Roger talked. Meanwhile, Roger looked first at Helena and then down at Ellen, not sure where his interest should light.

We talked about an exhibition at the Royal Academy in Burlington House which had generated a lot of controversy.

"I have some catalogs and reproductions I picked up in the bedroom," I said. Helena and Roger decided to settle a dispute by looking them over. The three of us retired to the bedroom. James remained on the sofa.

"Ellen," Fiona asked when they were alone, "will you do me a great favor?"

"Of course," said Ellen. "You and Etheria have been so kind to me I'd be happy to do whatever you want."

"I can't get up to London for the Victorian jewelry sale at Thwaites on June fifth. I will be in Edinburgh and there is a brooch in the sale I very much want. Will you bid on it for me?" Fiona produced a catalog from her capacious purse. "I have marked the lot number and I would be prepared to spend £350. I will tell Thwaites you are my agent and you can charge the brooch to my account if you get it."

Ellen took the catalog and smiled her radiant smile. "I'd be delighted to bid for you. It will be fun."

"Thank you," said Fiona.

The bell rang.

I spoke into the intercom. Weatherby announced himself. He would wait below for Helena and Fiona.

"Good-bye, James darling," said Helena, patting her devoted

friend. James gave her a devastatingly sad look. "My dear, it is not terrible. Look, it has made friends of Fiona and me," said Helena.

James groaned.

We said farewells and Helena and Fiona left. Roger and Ellen remained.

Roger, though his business is money management, is interested in the arts and is very knowledgeable. We happily talked for some time and Ellen looked decorative and seemed interested. Her softly curling hair swung back and forth across her charming face as she twinkled at Roger.

James was watching the performance. He seemed more alert, less absorbed in his sinfulness. He hopped off the sofa and moved closer to Ellen, who now sat on the floor next to the easy chair where Roger was sitting. At last James came close enough to flick Ellen on the leg with his tail.

She jumped up, her eyes wide, her lip curled in anger. Then she walked to the window, her back to us.

It was getting late. "Let's go to Colombino's for dinner," I suggested.

"Splendid idea!" said Roger. "I'll take you all."

"No, indeed," I said, meaning it.

"I want to," said Roger, who was, I would discover, a generously impulsive man when he wasn't being a calculating machine.

Ellen gave him a melting smile. "Wonderful idea," she said. "By the way, what happens to what's-his-name here?"

"Want to come too?" I asked James. "You know they love to see you at Colombino's."

James was about to shake his head.

"You mean you'd take him with us?" asked Ellen in angry surprise.

James stood up and nodded his head.

The four of us walked the two and a half blocks to the restaurant and we had a pleasant dinner, though Ellen kept looking at James uneasily as he lapped up marinara sauce from a small bowl and drank part of my red wine. After dinner we put Ellen into a taxi and Roger disappeared into the underground, while James and I walked back to Baron's.

Mrs. March was waiting for us outside my door. James was stomping along.

"You don't like Ellen much, do you?" I said at the door.

James shook his head and plodded upstairs, carrying the weight of the world's troubles on his shoulders.

The next morning James was back at his table screening arrivals. He seemed a little less gloomy but he was still very serious indeed. He barely gave me a nod as I left for the British Museum reading room.

However, he did come scratching at my door about four o'clock in the afternoon, and he had barely arrived when the intercom rang and I heard a voice say, "Shep has arrived."

"Come right up," I said, delighted. "Shep Wolf is here," I called to James.

Shep Wolf, whose real name is Marion Shepard Wolf, is a television producer. He is a particular friend of James's, because last year he produced a version of "Puss-in-Boots" that starred James himself. The program received excellent reviews and for a very brief time James was a celebrity. Shep is a tall, heavy man with black curly hair and a booming voice. He and James love to roughhouse together, and I was particularly delighted because he might be able to lighten James's mood where none of the rest of us had been able to.

We went together to open the door. There was Shep filling the hall, dressed as usual in jeans and a sheepskin jacket. In addition he had brought with him Poppy Balsom, a scene and costume designer. Auburn-headed Poppy is Helena's best friend. She is very good at what she does, but she has some eccentric ideas about the world, refuses to take jobs when she disapproves of the management, even though she desperately needs the money, and is prone to join protest marches just for the sake of marching. She is also, like Helena, a warm, sensitive and delightful woman. To us all she is a beloved friend despite her occasional odd behavior.

Shep bounded in, picked up James and threw him in the air, catching him easily. James was taken aback, but before I knew it he began to purr for the first time in days, and then he and Shep yowled together until I cried, "Stop, both of you!"

We had barely settled, Shep in the big chair, his long legs stretched out and James on his lap, when the bell rang again and Roger announced himself.

"Good," said Shep when I reported who was on the way up. "I asked him here especially."

I opened the door to Roger.

"You're Ham," said Shep, leaping to his feet and dumping James on the floor.

Poppy, who was curled up in a corner of the sofa, gave Roger her lively smile.

The two men were an interesting contrast. Shep seemed to fill any room he was in. Roger is not short, but he is slight and might have been overwhelmed. He has authority, however, and the two met as equals.

I presented Poppy. Shep returned to his chair. James returned to Shep's lap. I went to the kitchen and returned with drinks. I looked at James inquiringly.

"Want a Laphroaig?" I asked.

James thought for a minute, sighed and nodded and at last grinned.

Now we were all settled, James on the coffee table with a saucer of whiskey. Next to him was a plate of smoked oysters and some raw vegetables. He ignored the vegetables.

"Now shut up, everyone," said Shep. "I have collected this group for a purpose. I propose to produce a sequel to that wildly successful musical called *Cats*. This one is to be called *Cats International* and I propose to put it on in the Cottesloe Theater at the National Theater complex. I want James to help direct and I was hoping Roger might invest some of his money."

James opened his eyes wide, let out a yowl and began jumping up and down in Shep's lap.

"Careful there," said Shep, holding James at arm's length. "I take it you agree to help direct."

James nodded, grinning as widely as he could.

"This request does not come as a surprise," said Roger. "I guess Poppy here told Helena." Poppy nodded. "Helena told me during the tournament. I made some phone calls and did a little investigation, and since I have been wanting to speculate in the theater anyway, this seems a splendid way to start."

"Helena must have said some nice things about me," said Shep.

"She said you were a very vigorous fellow who bounded about a bit but that you were a very talented director and a shrewd producer."

Shep grinned. "She did, eh?"

He might have said more, but the bell rang again. I spoke into the intercom.

"It's Ellen here," I heard.

"Well, come up," I said, not entirely graciously.

I let her in. "Hello, Roger," she said, giving him her devastating smile.

I introduced Poppy and Shep. Ellen slipped to the floor next to Roger with a graceful movement. James hissed softly. Ellen ignored him.

"Roger," she said, "how wonderful to see you again. I was up the street at Fortnum's and just thought I'd stop in and say hello. I'd no idea there would be all these people here."

We gave her a drink, told her all about the new production with James as consultant, Poppy as designer, Shep as director-producer and Roger as angel. Finally, we all went off to Frank's for dinner where James ate fettuccine Alfredo, and Roger was maneuvered into picking up Ellen's check while the rest of us paid our own. Roger had as usual offered to take us all, but Poppy is adamant about paying her own way and would not hear of it. She offered to pay Ellen's check when Ellen found herself unexpectedly out of money, but Roger intervened.

James is a very fastidious cat and his table manners are impeccable, but I did notice that somehow he managed to flick cream and butter on Ellen's sleeve. I made no comment, however.

By the end of the evening we had made some practical arrangements. Roger and Shep had settled the money questions, and I had agreed to bring James to the rehearsal hall at the theater in two weeks.

James was much more himself, but I noticed an underlying sadness in him as he walked upstairs that night. His tail was dragging. I ached for him.

The next afternoon brought news from another quarter. James had been spending the afternoon with Peter Hightower and the two of them stopped in about five for refreshment. I poured La Iña sherry for Peter and a little Laphroaig for James and me and produced with no great effort some fine, ripe Stilton cheese and crackers for us all. James loves the cheese and ignores the crackers but finds them a useful substitute for a plate as he can sit on the windowsill and eat cheese off crackers with ease.

They were both full of excitement.

"I was going over the Dresden correspondence," said Peter. "It is, as was most of the correspondence of the time, a collection of business letters. Often the letter was simply a report of current prices, or a report of prices received for goods shipped or sometimes a report of the state of an account. This correspondence is no different. The contents of the letters is of interest to a historian who is interested in what things cost at a particular moment in history, or a record of the flow of goods in a given area. Since there were no envelopes at the time, the outside of the letter carries the address and any markings applied. I was reading the letter and sorting those with interesting route markings while James was sorting for forgeries on the big table. I had laid a letter down beside me, address side up, and suddenly James was patting my arm."

James turned a big grin to me and nodded. He was too excited to sit still so he began pacing across the back of the sofa.

"He called my attention to a mark on the paper. I looked at it carefully and it appeared it might be made up of the initials L-F. R."

It was my turn to be excited. "Did you find such a mark on Colonel Hargrave?" I asked.

James stopped pacing and nodded happily.

"There is more," Peter continued. He and James were exchanging conspiratorial looks. James was waving his tail back and forth.

"A little later on I came across a real letter, not just a list of prices. At the bottom of an accounting, the accountant writes, 'My nephew has come to stay with me and study sculpture. He seems a proper young man.' I'm giving you a translation from the German, of course."

"This certainly looks promising," I said. "On the other hand we may be misreading this small, casual remark, and any number of uncles have nephews come to visit."

James, who was extremely irritated that I was not instantly convinced, refused to join us when Peter and I went out to dinner. He stomped upstairs, flicking his tail at me as he went.

"Dear old James, he still is touchy these days, isn't he?" Peter mused.

The day of the sale of Victorian jewelry at Thwaites dawned without rain. To my surprise, James was at my door early. He came in as I opened it to get the morning paper. He was looking businesslike and he hurried me along. I had not planned to go to the sale as there was nothing in it I was interested in, but James was insistent and I had the time so off we went, James leading the way. When we got to the auction room I waited at the door to see what James would do. He picked a seat in a corner in the back and I joined him. I noted two people I knew in the hall. Down near the front was Ellen Bruce. Halfway back was Roger Ham. Neither noticed me.

The auction started. Items were offered and sold, generally for pretty good prices. I was getting bored, but James would not let me go. He sat on my lap. A Victorian brooch in the shape of a thistle with an amethyst blossom and tiny diamonds at the end of each of the thistle's thorny leaves was displayed. It was sold without incident to paddle nineteen, held by Ellen Bruce, for £200.00.

James, his eyes on Ellen, urged me to get up and leave, and, interpreting correctly that we were to follow Ellen inconspicuously, I did just that.

Since no items can be picked up until all the items consigned to the session have been auctioned, Ellen had some time to wait before she could claim her brooch. James had disappeared, but I realized I was to watch and wait and remain unseen.

Ellen slowly made her way down the stairs from the hall. As she did so, an elderly dealer I recognized was frantically hurrying up to one of the Thwaites men stationed at the door. There was a brief discussion and the Thwaites man pointed to Ellen, who was about to leave the building. The harried dealer went hurrying after her, and I moved into a position where I could see what was going on in the street.

Not only was it not raining, it was actually sunny, and Ellen was standing on the sidewalk enjoying the sun. The dealer had found her, introduced himself, and was involved in a deep discussion which I could not overhear. Practically at their feet, though unnoticed, was a grey cat asleep in the sun.

While I could not hear the conversation, it seemed a fair guess that the dealer wanted the thistle brooch and had been too late to bid on it. Perhaps he was now trying to buy it from Ellen.

At first Ellen looked irritated, but she had time to kill so she listened and very shortly she looked not irritated at all. At last she smiled a dazzling smile, they shook hands, the dealer flagged a cab and Ellen returned to the back of the hall to wait for the sale to end. She looked very happy indeed. The sale ended shortly. I looked around for James, but he had disappeared.

As soon as she could, Ellen went to the cashier's desk to pay in cash for her purchase. The brooch was placed in a velvet Thwaites box. Ellen wrapped a rubber band around it and started to put the box in her handbag. As she did so, something tripped her. She dropped the handbag and the contents spilled out on the floor. Ellen nearly fell, and she struggled to regain her balance. The area was full of people coming and going, paying for purchases and leaving Thwaites. Roger came by and bent to help Ellen pick up the contents of her purse. There was noise and confusion.

"Here," he said, "I'll help you," and he scooped up lipstick, keys, wallet, handkerchief, and whatever else he could find and returned the bag to the confused girl.

"What a shame," said Roger. "Let's get out of here, and I'll take you to Wilton's around the corner for lunch."

For a moment Ellen looked confused. Then she smiled her dazzler at him and walked out on his arm. She did not check the contents of her purse herself. She wanted to be on her way. After all, Wilton's is one of the most elegant and expensive restaurants in London.

"I do love Wilton's," she said as they left Thwaites.

I looked around for James. He was nowhere to be seen. I went off with friends, and it was not until the next afternoon that I heard a scratch at my door and opened it to find James sitting on an envelope and, strangely enough, a Thwaites box with a rubber band wrapped around it.

"Come in, I'm delighted to see you," I said. James swaggered in. He grinned, then he headed directly to the windowsill where he sat looking out. I put the box on the table and opened the envelope, which contained a note telling me that the Honorable Fiona Wettin had called to say she would be at my apartment at five-thirty and that I should expect Ellen Bruce at the same time.

I turned to James and pointed to the box. "Is that what I think it is?" I asked.

James hopped off the sill and onto the table. He nodded gleefully.

"I think Ellen is going to be surprised," I said. I thought of the scene on the street. "How much did the dealer offer her?" I asked. I held up three fingers, James shook his head. "More?"

James nodded. I held up four fingers. James shook his head. I held up my whole hand. James nodded.

"Wow," I said. "He was willing to pay £500 for that ugly thing."

The bell announced the arrival of Fiona, Ellen and Roger.

We greeted one another. Fiona rapidly looked around. She immediately saw the Thwaites box on the table and without a word more to anyone she picked it up, removed the rubber band and opened it. The brooch gleamed.

"Thank you, dear," she said to Ellen without taking her eyes off the jewel. "It is just as handsome as I knew it would be and Etheria will be delighted."

Ellen had turned pale. She opened her mouth and then closed it. She looked at the box and then at James, who was sitting on the table purring softly.

"Ellen, you look sick," said Roger. He seemed concerned.

"I'm all right," said Ellen weakly.

"Well," said Fiona, "I'm sorry I cannot stay but I have a train to catch. Thank you for doing this small service for me, Ellen." And she was out the door and on her way before we knew it.

Ellen sank into a chair. She looked totally exhausted.

"You really don't look well," said Roger. "I think I should take you home."

"Oh, Roger, would you? I really feel terrible," Ellen whispered.

"Sorry, James," said Roger. "I'll see you both soon, but I'm afraid I really should take her home."

We agreed and watched at the door as they descended in the tiny elevator, Ellen resting her head against Roger's shoulder.

Once they had left the building James let out a great meow

and bounded back into the sitting room. He rolled on the floor in glee.

I stood in the middle of the room looking at him. I began to see the light.

"James," I said sternly, "you stole the brooch from her purse when it spilled. You carried it back here in your mouth. In fact, you tripped her to make it fall."

James sat up and nodded and then rolled over again on his back and patted his paws together in applause.

"So, thanks to you, Fiona got her brooch and Ellen did not make £300 on the deal."

James stopped congratulating himself long enough to nod.

"And," I speculated aloud, "she won't be £200 out of pocket—it can still be charged to Fiona's account."

James was now up on the table lapping at the Laphroaig I had poured for him before the guests arrived. He then ate three anchovies off a cracker and broke into a dance on the table.

"James," I said very sternly, "you must realize that what you did was not in any way sporting. It is against the rules to steal. It is even against the law. If you are thinking about redemption, you cannot redeem the unsporting act of moving Fiona's ball at the tournament by stealing a brooch from Ellen to give to Fiona, even if you stole it from a girl who was breaking the rules herself."

James stopped dancing. He sat on the table and looked at me. Slowly the sense of what I was saying began to sink in. He looked wistful. Everything he did these days seemed to be wrong.

He jumped down from the table. He walked to the door. I opened it to let him out and met Mrs. March in the hall. He marched slowly up the stairs. He shook his head back and forth in a puzzled way.

"He looks gloomy tonight," said Mrs. March.

"He's had a hard day," I said. "Good night, James," I called. "You're still my best friend."

He did not turn around.

I hoped that, in time, James would come to regard his confrontations with the rules as a learning experience, but I could see, looking at the recent weeks from James's point of view, that all his friends had been distressed at every recent move he had made to be of service. He might just give us all up and that would be a grievous loss. However, bright and early the next morning, there was a scratch at the door and there was James. Not exactly bright eyed, but there, dragging his carry-bag. We were to go to the theater to begin rehearsals for *Cats International*.

"Good morning, Sir James," I said as I held the carry-bag open. James hopped in with a sniff. I picked up my umbrella and James, and we headed for the Green Park station. Once in the train, James looked around with interest. He dearly loves to create small disturbances among groups of punks, but the trip to Charing Cross on the Jubilee line was filled with businessmen and -women, nothing interesting. We changed at Charing Cross for the Northern line and rode to the Waterloo station. James did manage to scratch the jeans of a young man next to us who was doing his best to annoy a pretty girl, so I knew he was feeling better.

The National Theater complex is an imposing, not to say

intimidating, structure beside the river, and I had some trouble finding where we were supposed to go, but I asked frequently and at last James and I found the stage door, where at first the guard refused to let the cat come in. At last, in irritation, I pointed out that on the list of people to be admitted was the name James and beside it in blue pencil were the words "grey cat."

"All right," he said, "but if anything happens, it's not my fault."

James, who by this time was out of the bag, gave him a hiss and walked along beside me, his tail in the air. We wandered around a bit and at last found our rehearsal hall, where quite a crowd of people had assembled. The hall was simply a large room with a very high ceiling and a bare wood floor. Folding metal chairs were set up, and there was a table in one corner and an upright piano. There were also two mats of the sort used by gymnasts against one wall. The singers and dancers were dressed in leotards, sweaters and leg warmers. Shep, in his usual jeans with a black turtleneck shirt stood at one side with Poppy, who carried a clipboard and was wearing a dark green jumpsuit. Next to two comfortable director's chairs, one labelled SHEP and the other POPPY, was a high stool labelled JAMES. James sat on his stool and nodded to one and all. I pulled up a metal chair and joined the group.

The dancers now cleared the hall and began to warm up. James began scratching the top of the stool. A young acrobat moved out from the pack and began doing somersaults. James hopped off his stool and walked toward her. She stopped to look at the cat. He did a long front-paws stretch and turned to her. He waved a paw. She understood and, sitting on the floor, she repeated James's exercise. He shook his head and repeated the motion. She nodded and made some corrections on her own.

James nodded and they were off. They tried rollovers, back arches, pounces. Some movements took three or four tries to perfect, others were easy. The rest of the cast, Shep, Poppy and I all watched.

"Marvelous," said Shep at last. "I suggest that all of you try to follow Ursula and James. Some of you will not make all the movements. Don't worry about that, but get the feel."

So there was James, completing a movement and then watching as first Ursula and then the rest of the cast performed it.

While rehearsal was going on, the door opened and Roger came in.

"Hello, Ham," said Shep, "come to check on your investment?"

"I've come to learn something about the theater, now I've got money in it," said Roger, and sat down next to Poppy, who was sketching cat faces and costumes.

The door opened again and a round young woman with short, honey-colored curls came panting in.

"I'm sorry I'm late," she gasped. "I had no idea this place was so big or that there were three theaters, and I have been all over the place trying to find this rehearsal room. This feels almost like a city and I have been all over it."

"No harm done, Anne," Shep said. "We haven't really begun to set any business."

Roger took the opportunity to speak since the dancers had stopped working. "I want a show of hands," he said, "of those who have have never had a tour of this place."

I held up my hand. James held up a paw and to our surprise, most of the rest of the cast held up their hands as well.

"Very well," said Roger. "As angel, I insist that at the next break, say in an hour, Shep lead us on a tour of the place. Will you do that?" He turned to Shep.

"Splendid idea," said Shep. "Now, back to work."

The dancers went back to learning how to be cats, and shortly, Tony Duke, who was the choreographer, was turning the movements James had shown Ursula into a ballet. Anne, the roly-poly one, was having a very hard time with some of the movements, particularly those that were ideally adapted for tall, thin dancers. At last she gave up and sat on one of the mats in the corner and began to cry softly. James went to sit beside her. She stroked him and blew her nose. "If only I were tall and thin," she sighed to herself.

James stood up and tapped her on the leg to get her attention. She looked at him. He rolled over on his back, curled his paws and cocked his head to one side. She lay down on the mat and did the same. He rolled over, made a ball, tucked his paws under his chin and raised his haunches. She did the same. James sat up and patted the air. James was training a fat cat.

It was time for a break. The dancers put on sweaters and sat on the floor. An assistant who had arrived while everyone was at work passed out paper cups of fruit juice. Shep gave us five minutes' rest and then we started out in two groups to tour the complex. Our first visit was to the Oliver Theater, the largest of the three theaters housed here. It was dark, of course, until performance time but Shep found the work lights, and we saw a steeply pitched amphitheater of seats and an elaborate stage with moving sections that can go around or up and down. As a group, we sat in front-row seats while Shep pushed buttons backstage and James sat on the movable parts as they went round and round or up and down. He loved going down below the stage level and waving his tail as he disappeared.

Our next stop was the medium-size, conventional theater called the Lyttelton. It had seats pitched at the usual level, a proscenium arch and an orchestra pit, and it appeared to be in use at the moment. The curtain was open and a work light on. As we sat and watched, a very imposing black man appeared and crouched down in what appeared to be a very scruffy, dusty clump of grass on one side of the stage. He began roaring. Shep moved onto the stage. James went with him.

"Harry Kinyata," Shep called.

From somewhere out of sight, a voice called "Just a minute," and a flood of rosy light from the left and pale green light from the right brought the dirty clump of grass to vivid life. The man let out another roar and stood up. A technician made a slight adjustment in the lights.

"Fine," Harry called. Then the lights went out, leaving the work light.

Harry came to the front of the stage. "Hello, Shep," he said, holding out his hand. "What brings you here? I thought you were working down in number two."

"We are," said Shep, "but most of the dancers have never been around this place, so we're on an impromptu tour. What are you doing?"

"Well," Harry Kinyata now addressed all of us. "The producers of this piece think of it as an African revue. It is called *Hunt the White Hunter*. It has the usual idiot plot to be found in a revue, but it provides a vehicle for African dances and African music. We open in three weeks with a cast that is almost entirely African." During this small speech Harry was addressing the public. He has a wonderfully flexible voice and great presence and we felt the power of an outstanding personality. Suddenly he changed.

"By the way, Shep," he said in a perfectly ordinary voice, "you might be able to help me. I desperately need a young woman who should be attractive but need not be talented, to appear from time to time to identify a scene or character. I've been so caught up in getting my Africans acclimated in this cold, miserable country, I almost forgot about this one piece of casting."

"I know just the girl," said Roger from the audience.

"Who?" said Shep, who hadn't even had time to give the matter any thought.

"A girl named Ellen Bruce. She asked me if I could find a place for her in *Cats International*, but she is not much of a dancer and this might be just the thing for her. She's very good-looking."

"Well, send her around today if you can," said Harry. "I'll certainly take a look at her."

Then he turned to us, the audience. "I hope you all will find some time to come to our performance. The future of Africa, indeed the future of us all, depends on a greater understanding of our different cultures, and such exchanges as this go a long way toward making that possible." He bowed and turned to find James in the grassy clump. James let out a yowl. Harry let out a roar. James pounced. Harry pounced back. The curtains slowly closed. There was a scuffling sound and James crawled under the curtain and swaggered back to us, happily waving his tail.

Our tour took us through restaurants, exhibition areas where art shows were held from time to time, through a book shop, and wide halls. Then we left the public areas and were conducted through the backstage complex of rehearsal halls, costume and scene design areas, where the costumes were made and stored and scenery constructed and stored. There are a large number of dressing rooms and offices and at last we arrived at the Cottesloe Theater, the little theater of the three, where *Cats International* would make its debut. Cottesloe is a small (for a theater) rectangular space. Everything in the space is movable except the floors of the two balconies on three sides of the rectangle. The seats can be arranged in any way desired. For our production they would be arranged around the sides, and the performers would work in the middle. The side walls and ceiling of the space were painted black and seemed to disappear along with the pipes to which the multitude of lights were attached.

James was enchanted with the space, and while we sat on the floor in the center and listened to Shep outline the limitations of the performance, James danced along the pipes overhead, his silver fur glinting in the working lights.

Anne waved at him. He jumped down and landed in her lap. Delighted with this effort, he ran up the pipes, found another spot and sailed through the air to her lap again.

"Now," said Shep, "starting next week, I will have the size of this space taped on our rehearsal room floor, and we will go to work in earnest with Tony and the music."

We returned to rehearsal hall two.

As the dancers were getting ready to go to work again, James beckoned to Anne. She followed him. He walked up to Tony Duke, who is a lean, agile man with wispy grey hair.

"What's up, James?" Tony asked.

James sat down and waved a paw at Anne. Anne gulped and went through her new repertoire of fat cat movements. In the beginning she was self-conscious but she began to enjoy herself and Tony began to grin.

"Hey, Shep," he called, "come see this."

Anne performed again.

"We'll make her a character," said Shep, delighted. "She and Ursula will be splendid foils for each other."

Tony smiled at Anne, then he looked at James. "You are a clever fellow," he said. James nodded casually. After all, people were telling him he was clever every day. I was secretly delighted that James had, at least for the moment, become absorbed in the theater. He was certainly almost his old, insouciant self.

It was a long, hard day. We broke for lunch, which James and I had in the rehearsal hall because Shep had not been able to persuade any of the restaurant managers that a cat was the technical director of a production. In the end he brought us tuna fish sandwiches and cartons of milk. James didn't mind much. He had worked harder, physically, all morning than he ever does, and he went to sleep immediately after eating the tuna out of a sandwich. I took the opportunity to visit the office of the costume department, where Poppy showed me the sketches she had already done for some of the cats. She and an engineer were working on the problem of the cats' tails. They hoped, through a series of straps and strings, to be able to control the tails and give them catlike movements.

During the afternoon some music was added and Tony devised some exercises he expected his dancers to do to make the catlike movements they must perform more accurate. This required James to repeat many movements a number of times, and he stretched and pounced and arched his back and ran across the floor most of the afternoon.

On the way home, he paid almost no attention to anyone in the crowded train. At last, we were safely back in flat twelve. I poured a little Laphroaig in James's saucer and some in a glass with a little water for myself and had just settled down when the bell rang and Roger announced he was there with Ellen. James barely opened an eye.

Ellen had recovered her self-possession. She sat on the floor at Roger's feet.

"She got the job," Roger announced. "Harry Kinyata was quite taken with her. Your career is on its way," he said, ruffling her hair.

I noticed a slight twitch of distress on her face at Roger's gesture, but she smiled happily at him.

I heard a slight hiss, but James appeared to be sound asleep.

When we went out to dinner, he declined and walked wearily up the stairs but I noted he seemed just tired, not depressed.

Life now changed drastically for James. He spent most of his time at the theater supervising the rehearsals of *Cats International*, so he spent less time than he used to at Thwaites and almost no time checking out the tenants at Baron's.

As I was leaving one morning, one of the maids, María, met me in the hall.

"That couple in flat eleven is truly dirty," she said. "I can't imagine how they ever got in here. James spots that type right away. They have paid in advance so we can't throw them out, but they are awful."

Each afternoon when James came back from the theater, he was truly tired, but the workout was doing him good. He was a leaner, trimmer cat.

The very afternoon of the day María had spoken to me, I was determined to mention the matter to James, but Roger and Ursula had come to my flat with James and he was busy showing them how he could walk on the windowsill on his hind legs. Of course, since Roger was there, Ellen had followed. She was talking at some length about how hard it was for a girl of exceptional breeding to get along with no money.

At last, James could stand it no more. He jumped off the windowsill, trotted over to Ellen where she sat on the floor at Roger's feet and smacked her on the mouth with his paw.

Ellen looked greatly startled and said no more.

Ursula said good-bye and left.

"I guess I'd better get you fed," said Roger.

"How lovely," said Ellen, leaping to her feet. "Can we go to Mon Plaisir?"

"I guess so," said Roger without enthusiasm. "I really had something simpler in mind."

Ellen has selective deafness and she was already on the phone making a reservation.

"They'll take us if we hurry," she said.

"Fine," said Roger cheerfully. "Come along, you two."

"Oh, dear," said Ellen, not at all distressed, "they only have room for two."

"Then we'll go someplace else," said Roger.

Ellen looked really distressed.

"Go on," I said. "James is exhausted and we'll have a bowl of soup right here. I'll see you at rehearsal tomorrow."

They left, Ellen beaming triumphantly.

"James," I said, "do you think Roger really likes Ellen?"

James shook his head. He shrugged his trim shoulders and yawned a huge yawn.

"Want some soup?" I asked.

He shook his head. He walked to the door. I opened it. He turned on the stairs and waved a paw at me. He was nearly his old self.

The next day I took James to the theater. The rehearsals had been going very well and only the finale was left to be finally set. Poppy wanted my opinion on some patterns she was using on the set. *Cats International* was one of her few forays into set design as well as costume.

We were in rehearsal room two. The man at the upright piano played an introduction and the dancers assembled for the finale. James, carried away by the music, joined the dancers. He knew all the steps—after all he had invented many of them—and he danced with Ursula and Anne in front of the rest. He was a fluid, grey streak of movement, arching, stretching, pouncing, playing with an imaginary ball. As the music became more insistent, he climbed a flat that was leaning against the wall and, inspired by the crescendo as the music rose to a climax, he launched himself into the air and landed safely on a beanbag chair, used as a prop in the scene.

There was a burst of spontaneous applause. James grinned, then assumed a modest attitude, but he clearly was delighted with the opportunity to show off.

"That would make the most spectacular finale," said Shep, slinging James on his shoulder. "We could introduce him a little earlier. What do you think, Tony?"

James slipped off Shep's shoulder and pranced over to Ursula and Anne, who were sitting on the floor.

"We'll never look like James," Ursula was saying.

"I know it," said Anne sadly. "He's such a darling, but it does make the illusion that we are cats much harder to sustain." She stroked James affectionately.

"All right," said Tony, "let's try it again."

The dancers assembled. James sat on his stool.

"James," called Tony, "we need you."

James shook his head.

"You don't want to do it?" asked Shep.

James nodded. I thought for a moment he might change his mind, but he curled up on the stool and closed his eyes.

The rehearsal proceeded without him.

Some long time later, we sat in the sitting room watching the news on the tube. We had enjoyed a little whiskey and quite a lot of crab salad.

"You really wanted to do that part, didn't you?" I asked when the news was over.

James nodded.

"You heard Ursula and Anne talking?"

James nodded.

"You were right, you know, it will be better in the long run as an all-people show."

James nodded.

"You've done a superb job as consulting director."

James grinned.

"You're almost as good a sport as Helena," I said, hoping I was not touching too sore a spot.

James had been sitting at the other end of the sofa. He stood up, walked three steps, sat down next to me and worked his head under my hand, and we sat cuddled together, content.

Mrs. March knocked.

James jumped up. I opened the door. James ran out and sat on the stairs the way he used to do.

"Is James here?" asked Mrs. March.

"He's right over there," I said, pointing and laughing.

James gave me a wink and flirted his tail.

"He looks more like himself," she said happily. "I hope he hasn't been getting into mischief."

"No, indeed," I said and grinned happily.

Opening night came for *Cats International*. Roger provided seats for Helena, Lord Henry, James and me. He had elected to stay backstage with Poppy and Shep. James abandoned his seat early in the performance and sat on a light batten watching Anne and Ursula, so Ellen managed to usurp James's seat. The performance was a delight. The audience was unusually enthusiastic, and even before the reviews were out everyone knew the production was a huge success.

Roger hosted a post-performance opening night party in the grill room of the Cafe Royale. James was tempted to climb the baroque carving surrounding the mirrors that line the walls of this restaurant but instead rode on Shep's shoulder and looked at himself in the mirrors. I took the opportunity to tell Helena how James had decided not to perform in the finale.

"Wise James," she said, as he collapsed beside her after having been tossed in the air by Shep. "Not many actors I know would voluntarily give up a splendid part they had been offered for the good of the show. I'm proud to know you."

James gave Helena a long wistful look.

"James," she said seriously, "you are one of my very best friends. You always were and you always will be."

At that moment Roger proposed a toast to Shep for his inspired concept. Tony followed this with a toast to James for his choreography. James stood on the table on his hind legs and waved both paws. Roger tried to propose a toast to Poppy Balsom for her stunning set, costumes and makeup, but Ellen managed to distract him and Lord Henry made the toast instead. The BBC had covered the opening night and the party as well, and the next day James and I could see him riding on Shep's shoulder on the morning news. He was not greatly impressed. After all, he had been on television before. However, I was delighted to see he was his old enthusiastic, intelligent self. The pall of guilt and self-reproach that had hung over him since the tournament had lifted. He was a cat redeemed.

He spent the morning checking on new tenants at Baron's and the afternoon at Thwaites with Marilyn sorting Persian forgeries from genuine stamps while I went off to have a meeting with the curator of the Huntingdown Museum, a treasure trove of eighteenth-century painting and sculpture with a few pieces from the earliest Christian period. The director is Costain Cummings, a ponderous chap who takes a long time to get to the point when he talks, but who is enormously respected in museum circles for his knowledge and integrity. The Huntingdown Museum is housed in a charming Georgian mansion. In the garden at the back, in what were once the stables, is a gift shop where reproductions of pieces of sculpture in the museum are for sale as well as prints of the most interesting paintings and art books.

The original collection was made by a Miss Huntingdown, and it has a reputation as one of London's small but choice museums. I have known Costain Cummings for some years, and when I got to London I called him to tell him of my foolish search. I had just heard from him. He had at his museum a terra-cotta maquette, or small model, of a marble statue of the actor David Garrick as Shakespeare done by Roubiliac. This statue had come on loan to the Huntingdown for study from the art collection of the Folger Shakespeare Library. He thought I might like to see it. Since it was just such a model for some other Roubiliac sculpture I was hoping against hope to find, I would indeed. I had gone to the Victoria and Albert Museum to see a marble statue of George Friedrich Handel by Roubiliac, but I had been unable to examine it closely. I particularly wanted to take James with me as he was the only one who had seen the monogram.

One morning early, a few days after the opening of *Cats International*, James found time in his busy schedule to go to the museum with me, so I took him in a cab in the carry-bag to the Huntingdown. The museum was not open for visitors at that early hour of the morning, but the guard at the door had been alerted that I would be there with a large bag, and I was shown to the curator's office, where I introduced James.

"It is with the greatest pleasure indeed that I meet the illustrious Sir James," said Costain, starting to bend to the floor to shake James's paw. James hopped on Costain's desk and they shook.

"Now, without further ado, and dispensing with ceremony, I will come right to the point and show you the terra-cotta model our fine sculptor made of the Shakespeare marble. Of course, it does not resemble Shakespeare as many people think he looked because it is really a portrait of David Garrick, the great actor and friend of Joshua Reynolds and Samuel Johnson, but it is a really fine piece of work, as I'm sure you will agree."

At last he stopped for breath and produced from a large cupboard beside him a beautiful statue about eighteen inches tall, superbly detailed, dramatic in feeling and full of life. What a splendid craftsman was L-F. R. I began to wish there were more of these handsome pieces. James sat on the desk and examined the piece with great care. At last he looked at me and nodded. Then he pointed his paw at the bottom edge of the statue and there, at the base, almost hidden by the sole of Shakespeare's foot was the tiny monogram L-F. R.

"I will be happy to consult with my colleague at the V and A and suggest that he send a minion to find the monogram on the Handel statue. I am sure it is there. That will give you an additional assurance. Is there anything else I can do for you to assist you in your search?"

"Not at the moment," I answered, beginning to sound like Costain. "I will just have to wait until Peter Hightower's search of some Dresden correspondence is complete and then perhaps I will have a more substantial lead."

James listened to this exchange and let out a small yowl. He then solemnly shook hands with Costain Cummings and after many flowery protestations of friendship, we parted.

When we got back to Baron's, James insisted that I come up to the office. I said a cheery hello to Mrs. March, who was busy on the telephone. James pointed to a small reproduction of an Egyptian cat god, Bastet, wearing gold earrings, which I had gotten for him last year. I picked up the statue and next to it was a small box containing a pair of gold earrings.

"Want these, too?" I asked.

James nodded and bounded down the stairs to flat twelve. I let us in. I put the statue on the table and, as James insisted, I put the earrings on him, through the holes in his ears, which had been pierced for these very earrings last year. He stood on the back of the easy chair and looked at himself in the mirror. He grinned. He turned his head first this way, then that. He shook his head, making the earrings wave back and forth. He tried different expressions. At last, in an effort to see himself from around his shoulder, he fell off the back of the chair.

"Oh, James," I cried, picking him up and hugging him, "you are yourself again."

He squirmed out of my arms and began to pace up and down the windowsill to regain his dignity, but he couldn't carry it off and grinned his old evil mischievous grin.

With earrings in place, he went back to work, sitting on his table at Baron's for the rest of the day.

In the afternoon Helena, who had been up to see her doctor in London, where she and Lord Henry were taking Lamaze instruction on the birth of the heir, dropped in with him to be followed shortly by Roger and the ever-present Ellen.

I served tea to Helena and Ellen, and Laphroaig to James, Lord Henry, Roger and myself. James found some anchovies and little shrimps in sauce in the larder and we had those with crackers.

"No petits fours?" asked Ellen.

"Sorry," I said.

James sneered.

"You two see a lot of each other," said Helena pleasantly as Ellen wrapped one arm around Roger's knee.

"I do think Roger is absolutely wonderful," said Ellen, giving him a soulful look. "I just wish he would let me do more for him. Even if I am busy as the star of *Hunt the White Hunter*, I could do more for him but he just doesn't ask."

Roger looked uncomfortable.

"Dear me," said Ellen, looking at her watch, "we must be getting on if I am to have dinner and get to the rehearsal on time." She didn't actually say "Come on, Roger" but the words were in the air and Roger got up and took her off to dinner. He didn't even seem to mind it.

James sat on the windowsill and watched them go down the street. He sniffed.

"Bring Poppy around soon," I suggested.

James and Helena nodded to each other.

"I'll do what I can to bring those two together, but you know Poppy, she is so independent. She likes Roger very much, but she wishes he were poor, and she certainly is not interested in chasing him. It isn't her style," said Helena.

"It certainly is Ellen's style," said Lord Henry, and with that they left for Haverstock Hall.

We should all have had more confidence in Roger's good sense. He began to visit *Cats International* just before the performance while Poppy was checking makeup. He would sit and inspect the cast with her and then he would ask her out for supper. She went often but insisted on paying her own way.

"She's determined to take nothing from anyone," said Roger to me one day.

Then one day when it rained in the morning and the sun shone for three whole hours in the early afternoon only to turn gloomy in the late afternoon, Peter Hightower arrived and brought a very frail, old man who walked on thin legs with the help of a beautiful ebony cane. The cane had an ivory head carved in the shape of a bending woman. His thin frame was clothed in a handsome, if old-fashioned suit. His face was almost expressionless but his blue eyes were alert.

I helped him into the apartment and settled him in the easy chair.

"Let me introduce Herr Hendler," said Peter.

The old man inclined his head and I bowed. James sat on the coffee table and looked dignified. His earrings, which he wore all the time now, gleamed in the lamplight.

"Would you like something to drink?" I asked. "Perhaps some tea, or sherry or whiskey?"

There was a gleam in the old man's eyes. "Sherry, please," he said. Peter joined him and I poured whiskey for James and myself, and then I sat down to wait for Peter to elucidate.

"Herr Hendler is the man who sent us the Dresden correspondence, which, it appears, we will auction sometime in September. It is a real treasure and should bring very good prices."

Herr Hendler's eyes gleamed. He sipped his sherry.

"However, we are not here to talk about the collection. It appears that Herr Hendler is a direct descendant on his mother's side of the uncle of L-F. Roubiliac."

Herr Hendler nodded and finished his sherry. I refilled his glass. He smiled a cracked smile.

"It appears that L-F. stayed and worked in Dresden and after some years migrated to England, where he became very successful."

"Very successful," echoed Herr Hendler in a heavily accented, barely audible voice.

"Would you like to tell the story?" asked Peter.

"*Nein*," said the old man. I guessed his English was not very fluent.

"It appears," Peter continued, "that sometime in the 1750s our boy sent two terra-cotta models of statues he had completed in marble to his uncle as gifts. These pieces, each about twenty-four inches high, were taken to Argentina when the branch of the family that had inherited them moved to Buenos Aires around 1910. These pieces may well still be in Argentina."

For a moment I didn't know what to say. So, as late as 1910, two models did exist. I was full of questions, but one look at Herr Hendler told me he would not be able to answer many. He was, at the moment, feebly trying to brush James off the back of the big chair. James, however, was still intent on admiring himself in the mirror and paid no attention.

Herr Hendler's eyes were growing dim. He put down his empty sherry glass. His hand trembled. He looked beseechingly at Peter. James bounced on the back of the chair to make his earrings shake.

Peter looked concerned and got up. "Do you want to go back to your hotel?" he asked. The old man nodded and struggled to his feet with my help. He shuffled to the elevator with Peter at his side.

"See you and James tomorrow," Peter called as the elevator descended slowly.

James and I returned to the flat. I was almost dancing. James looked puzzled.

"I've found them," I crowed. "Two models."

James shook his head.

"Well, no," I agreed. "I haven't found them yet, but I'm closer."

The next morning we went to Thwaites, where James waved a paw and went to find Marilyn while I stopped off to talk to Peter in his office.

"Herr Hendler is certainly feeble," I said as I sat down.

"And perhaps, last night, just a little drunk," said Peter. "He loves good sherry. But back to the story. He suddenly decided to sell this correspondence, which has been in his family for generations. He wants to be able to divide the proceeds himself rather than let his children fight over it. I only hope he lasts till after the sale. He is very happy with us here at Thwaites, so he is going home tomorrow."

"How will I find out the name of the Argentine family?" I asked with some anxiety.

"Never fear," said Peter confidently, "I'll get it out of one of his children. His oldest son particularly, who is getting on in years himself, is eager to have the material sold and is trying to be very helpful. I will get the answer from him soon."

When I left Thwaites I was euphoric. It appeared the impossible might come true. I called Costain Cummings and told him the news.

"If it should befall that you do indeed lay your hands on the two models, be good enough to let me see them and photograph them for our archive, will you?"

"If my principal agrees, I'll do so gladly," I answered. "We'll be in touch."

I went off for dinner with a group of dealers.

Next morning when I opened my door I found María's cart, on which she carries linen, towels and cleaning equipment, in the hall outside flat eleven, which is next door to mine. The door to the flat was open and María and James were looking at a sinkful of dishes. Clothing was strewn all over the apartment. A towel had been used to clean a pair of black leather shoes. It was covered with shoe polish. Nail enamel had hardened on the wash basin in the bathroom.

James was looking unhappy. Clearly these people should never have been accepted.

"Funny," said María as she started to pick up the used towels. "People this messy are always the first to get mad if you leave any dirt in the apartment."

James pricked up his ears. Then, his eyes partially closed, he left the apartment purposefully. I went out about my business.

In the early afternoon I was in my apartment studying an auction catalog in preparation for bidding when I heard a noise in the hall. Out of curiosity and because I was bored, I peeked out the door to find a very untidy woman in an angry conversation with María.

"You certainly didn't clean the room," she said harshly. "There was this white powder all over the rug in the sitting room."

María, who comes from Spain but speaks excellent English, looked helpless. "*No hablo inglés,*" she said. "*No entiendo.*"

"Oh, for God's sake," said the woman and slammed her door. I opened mine a bit more and winked at María. She winked back.

James spent the next day at Baron's and about four in the afternoon I heard something at my bathroom window. I opened it to find James stepping very carefully into the bathtub. I ran a little water in the tub, just enough to make a pool at the end, and James delicately washed a combination of jam and soot off his front paws. He then flicked the plug chain, unplugged the tub and stepped out onto a towel I had laid on the floor for him. He sat on the towel and licked himself into shape.

In the hall I heard shouts of anger. I opened the door a crack.

"We're leaving!" I heard coming from upstairs.

Mrs. March murmured something I could not hear. She never yells.

"The week we paid for is up and I will not stay here longer."

"Just come down and look," the woman yelled. "There are towels strewn all over the place and some sticky black tracks on my clothes, and in the tub—a mouse, a dead mouse."

James was now standing beside me. I gave him a long look, then I began to laugh. "Splendid," I cried.

He gave me a wink and began to roll on the floor.

"A dead mouse in the tub, that really wasn't nice," I said, trying to be stern. It was no use. I was rocking on the sofa laughing. Shortly Mrs. March and María appeared, wreathed in smiles. We all celebrated with a little sherry. Then Mrs. March went back to the office, María went off to clean the apartment and James went off to supervise.

That night James and I spent comfortably together. We ate curried chicken with chutney and had some white wine and then watched the news. It was the last quiet night for some time to come.

The next morning Peter Hightower called to report that a certain Augustus Hendler had indeed gone to Buenos Aires in 1902 to establish an accounting firm. It took only a little effort to find the Argentine Embassy office in London. I received helpful attention and I was supplied with the name and address of R. Hendler y Asoc., Contador, with offices in the Bank of Boston building on the corner of Florida and Av. Roque Saenz Peña in Buenos Aires.

I called Peter to report.

"Thwaites has a small office in Buenos Aires," said Peter, "with a perfectly charming fellow, Alberto Ocampo Dure, in charge. I know him and I'll call him today and see if he can find out anything. It will take a while—there's a four-hour time difference at this time of year."

"I'm very grateful," I said, "but I think I'll have to go and see what I can find out in person, whatever he says."

"I think so too," said Peter.

My next call was a long-distance one to the man who wanted to own the models. I reported my progress. He took no time to consider.

"Do whatever you have to in order to find those models if they still exist. Money is no object. And make life easy for yourself—go first class all the way," he said and hung up. He is like that. His name is George Leffingwell and he is known to many in the art world as "old G. L." for Got Lots, or, some irreverent souls say, "Gluttony Lust."

One problem remained: James. I needed him. I needed his eye to be sure of what I had. I would never have found those tiny monograms by myself. Mrs. March reluctantly agreed to let James go. I now had to smuggle him out of England, into Argentina, and back into England again. Perhaps the most difficult part would be the return to England because of its stringent quarantine rules.

Things were somewhat simplified when I discovered that British Airways had inaugurated a direct flight between London and Buenos Aires. I booked a first-class seat for the following evening. That night I discussed the trip with James. At first he was not very interested. I finally got Mrs. March to produce an old atlas. "Here we are in London," I said. "Tomorrow night we will get on an airplane and fly to Argentina, where it is winter. It will take all night. After breakfast we will arrive in Buenos Aires and go on to our hotel."

James nodded. His ears pricked up, and he began to look interested.

"Now I am sorry to say we are going to have to break the rules on this trip," I said. James grinned. "You see, the airlines will not let me take a cat with me and even if they would, England would not let you come back in without waiting in a kennel for three months and that would not do. So, with your help, I am going to smuggle you out of and back into the country. Do you want to try?"

James nodded, his eyes alert.

"Fine," I said and hoped it would be. "Remember, do exactly as I say whenever I give you a command."

James nodded impatiently. Did I think he was stupid?

I was secretly afraid of his impulsiveness.

Peter contacted Alberto Ocampo Dure, who was delighted at the prospect of a fine-art hunt, and he agreed to meet us at the airport and be our guide and companion during our stay. Now it would be a matter of luck.

I packed a bag I could carry onto the plane so I would not have to wait for luggage. I had no real problem with clothing. Even though it was winter in Buenos Aires, the temperature would be no colder than on a cool, rainy day in May in London. I took a topcoat and James in his carry-bag hidden by a sweater or two laid on top of him. I had forgotten all about security, but James had his own ideas and at last I deferred to his better judgment and let him out of the bag as soon as I knew the gate number. We walked together to the departure lounge. I was sitting with the somewhat hidden carry-bag open by my chair, when the boarding announcement came over the loudspeaker. I felt, rather than saw, a bulge in the bag. I placed my sweater over the top and heard the slightest purr.

In due time we were boarded. I placed the carry-bag at my feet. The first-class section was not full, so I had two seats to myself. I moved to the aisle seat and placed a blanket on the window seat. Soon, what looked like a pillow had grown under the blanket and when I lifted a corner two golden eyes peered at me. We took off. I relaxed.

We were served a quite acceptable dinner and I managed to share enough with James to make him comfortable. After dinner I helped him to a little of my brandy, and then I put on my sleep mask and James wrapped himself in the blanket and we ignored the movie. I slept pretty well, all things considered.

I was awakened early by a charming stewardess with orange juice. I picked up the carry-bag and headed for the lavatory.

"Sorry, James," I said, "that I can't give you more privacy but it's all we've got."

James just shrugged. He is, I discovered, an excellent traveller.

We landed. With James absolutely silent and immobile in the carry-bag, I walked through Immigration, had my passport stamped, received my visitor's pass and then proceeded through the nothing-to-declare line of Customs. No one paid any attention to me, and once through the barrier I was greeted by a very tall, curly-haired young man in a well-cut business suit holding a sign that read JAMES.

I waved to him. "Welcome," he said. "How was your flight and where is this James?"

"James is right here," I said, relieved that we had gotten to Buenos Aires without incident.

"Bring along the bag and the cat and I'll take you to your hotel," he said.

Once in the car, James wriggled out of the carry-bag and sat on my lap. I introduced him properly.

"I have booked you a room in the Claridge Hotel," said Alberto. "If you like, I can come up with you while you get settled and cleaned up, and I'll tell you what I know and then we can make plans."

"Splendid," I said, and this is what we did. The Claridge is a delightful hotel in downtown Buenos Aires, a block from Florida, a pedestrian street full of shops and beautiful baroque buildings. It was a cool day, but sunny. The downtown streets were full of people.

While I was dressing after my shower and James was stretching and grooming himself, Alberto filled us in on what he had discovered.

He knew the Hendlers. They were among the finest families in the city, and their business was very successful. The founder, Augustus, came with his wife to Buenos Aires in 1902 at the age of thirty-five. He had two children, Augustus II and Elizabeth, both born in Germany. Elizabeth never married and died in 1983 at the age of eighty-nine. Augustus II married an Argentine heiress. They had one child, Ricardo, now in his seventies. He comes to the office from time to time, but his son, Augustus III, who is now about forty, runs the business. Ricardo married the daughter of a wine maker in Mendosa, so the family has very extensive properties in the city of Buenos Aires and the surrounding countryside.

"Augustus III's children, who are in their teens and early twenties, spend a lot of time in Europe," Alberto continued. "Augustus III has a sister Elena. She never married and was particularly close to her great-aunt Elizabeth. That's the family. I regret to say they have such wealth that they buy at auctions rather than sell, and I can think of no reason why they would part with your models if they still have them. In fact, I don't know of a way we could even ask. Augustus III sometimes bids in London auctions on Victorian landscapes—I don't know why. If he wants something he buys it. Price is not a consideration. He has never offered anything through us or, as far as I could tell, through anyone else in England or the Continent. There is no market here."

I looked over at James. He had found a windowsill and was looking out over the rooftops of the city, taking it all in. It was a great day, crisp air, blue sky, glittering sun. A wonderful day to find yourself hopelessly defeated.

Alberto and I looked at each other for a few moments. Then he stood up and clapped his hands.

"I am taking the day off," he exclaimed. "You have come all these miles to my beautiful city. We will spend the day visiting it." He looked at his watch. "We will start out with a walk downtown to see the president's palace and the tomb of our liberator, San Martin, in the cathedral. Then we will proceed to a most unusual cemetery, called La Recoleta. After a visit there we will have a delicious luncheon at one of the restaurants nearby and then see what the afternoon brings."

There being nothing else to do, I agreed and the three of us set off on a walking tour of downtown Buenos Aires.

It is a beautiful city with splendid baroque buildings side by side with dreadful modern ones and an unusually large collection of handsome girls. The pink presidential palace was impressive and it was evident by the number of old churches that the country was largely Catholic. After a delightful walk we returned to the hotel and picked up Alberto's car. We drove through charming old streets till we reached a parking area in a park. We got out of the car and entered La Recoleta. We passed through white marble columns and found ourselves in a small city of stone tombs in the shape of houses. These tombs, called *bovedas*, are set as close together as possible along streets that meet at a boulevard that bisects the cemetery. This boulevard has cypress trees lining it and occasional stone benches. The bovedas all have doors with glass panes in them permitting anyone to look inside to see a small altar and, often, a casket or two.

Only the oldest and finest families of the country lie in this cemetery. While some of the bovedas are simple, most are very elaborate, with marble figures towering over the roofs. On the sides next to the doors are plaques in brass donated by friends, relatives and business associates of the deceased. Many presidents of Argentina are buried in bovedas, as are numerous generals and rich businessmen.

I was awed. I sat for a moment on one of the stone benches and listened to the silence. La Recoleta is not very large and the city bustles outside its four high walls, but no sound penetrates. It is very peaceful in the shade of the cypresses. I felt composed. I was almost beginning to feel reconciled to living a good life without the models when James, who had disappeared into the side streets, suddenly came racing down the main boulevard and tugged at my leg. Alfredo and I followed him down a side street, where we saw a middle-aged woman standing in front of a moderately elaborate boveda.

James stopped us. Then he walked very slowly up to the woman and stopped right next to her. He did not make a sound.

He just sat. She looked down at him. He was wearing his gold earrings and they glinted in the sun.

"You nice cat," she said. She reached down and patted James. He purred in a dignified way. "What attractive earrings you have," she said, and stroked him. He sat and purred. All of a sudden she sat on the stone street and hugged him. He melted into her arms.

"You are really a darling," she said. "You aren't a stray, I'm sure of that. You are so well fed and neat and you have those earrings on."

I saw James flick his tail and I motioned to Alfredo. We strolled along until we came to the woman and the cat.

"*Buenos días*," Alfredo said, and bowed.

"*Buenos días*," she replied, standing up with James in her arms and then, guessing I was English, said, "Good day."

"Good day," I said. "You speak English?"

"Oh, yes," she said, almost laughing, "and French and German, too."

I looked for a minute at James and saw that he was staring at the small altar that was visible through the door of the boveda. To my astonishment, on the altar were what appeared to be two terra-cotta statues about twenty-four inches high. One looked like a Scottish warrior, dressed in a kilt, with his arm upraised in a fierce gesture of attack. The other depicted a middle-aged man sitting on a bench playing a lyre in his bedroom slippers and nightcap.

I blinked. I looked again. They were still there. In the meantime the woman was stroking James and he was snuggling against her as though she were Helena.

"May we introduce ourselves?" I asked.

"By all means," she said. "I am Elena Hendler, a lonely old

woman feeling sorry for herself this morning. This is the Hendler boveda and I'm just going to put fresh flowers on the altar for Tante Elizabeth. I am the only one who cares anymore."

I gulped. Alfred, however, did the honors and introduced us all. "I'm glad you like James," he said. "He clearly doesn't think you are an old woman."

Miss Hendler smiled. She had a very nice smile that lightened her heavy features. She was a stocky woman in expensive but dull clothes and sensible walking shoes.

"Could we help, or at least keep you company while you refresh the flowers?" I asked.

"How nice of you. Then I can keep the cat a little longer."

She put James down and he sat quietly next to her. She took out a key and opened the door. In the center of the altar was a glass bowl full of dead flowers which she emptied. She had brought a pail full of fresh carnations and arranged them in the bowl as Alfredo and I watched. I was staring at the statues, more and more convinced that they were the ones we were looking for.

"Those pieces are quite interesting," I said in a neutral voice.

"Oh, them," she said angrily.

"You don't like them?" I asked.

"They are totally inappropriate. I do wish more than anything that I had a pair of white marble angels," she said. Then she replaced the bowl, closed the door and locked it.

Alfredo looked at his watch. "It is nearly lunchtime," he said. "Would you consider it at all possible to come as our guest for lunch? I'm sure it would give James great pleasure and give our visitor from England a chance for a conversation with a real Argentinian."

I thought she would refuse, but instead she smiled delightedly and said, "I should like that very much indeed." I bent to pick up the pail.

"Leave that," she said. "My maid will get it later. I like to arrange the flowers myself but she does the real cleaning."

"May I carry your cat?" she asked as an afterthought.

"Indeed, yes," I said. James adapted himself to her arms and purred happily.

We left La Recoleta and walked to a restaurant close by where Miss Elena was well known and catered to, and there was no question but that James was to have lunch with the rest of us.

"Shall we have a drink before we order?" Alberto asked.

"That would be nice," said Elena. "I should love a whiskey with ice, and none of your Argentine whiskeys."

"Johnny Walker black label?" Alberto asked.

"Splendid," said Elena, her sallow cheeks turning pink.

"Miss Hendler, I believe your father would prefer that you drink sherry," said the captain uneasily.

She waved him away. "Whiskey it is," she said, and whiskey it was.

All this time James had been sitting on her lap, purring very quietly. She stroked his soft fur from time to time.

"Would you like a taste of my drink?" she asked. James nodded gently and she poured a little whiskey on a plate. He lapped. She beamed at him.

The captain returned and we ordered an adequate lunch.

"Would you like some wine?" Alberto asked.

"Splendid!" said Elena, who had gotten quite pink by now. "But none of your Argentine stuff—either French or Chilean."

The captain looked very unhappy, but Alberto had been studying the wine list. He ordered by number and waved the captain away.

Then Miss Elena began to talk. Her life story—interrupted with occasional sips of whiskey and later a delicious Chilean white wine, comments to James, and, once, hiccups—was filled with frustration.

"I was born ugly to a mother who, like many Argentine women, was devoted to looking tall, thin and tanned. I was short and fat, and had pale skin that burned and peeled in the sun, so Mother paid no attention at all to me. My father left the children and the home to Mother, the way all Argentine men do. We two children saw him occasionally. My brother, who is tall and handsome, delighted my mother, but I found a friend, my great-aunt Elizabeth. She was short and blond and never went near the sun. She was ugly but very smart. She taught me French and English. I went to the German school, where we spoke German and Spanish. Of course, we spoke Spanish at home, but I enjoyed sometimes lapsing into French to annoy my mother." She grinned a most engaging grin.

So she grew up ignored by her parents. She spent her time with Tante Elizabeth, as she called her great-aunt. She became a devout Catholic, much more deeply committed to the Church than her parents or brother. At one point she wanted to become a nun, but her father would not permit it. As she grew older and it became evident that she would never marry, her father began to organize her life for her.

"He decides what I can eat, and drink, and where I can go." She grinned again. "You see, pussy, this lunch is special because he isn't telling me what to do."

So her days were filled with Tante Elizabeth and work for the Church. She watched her brother get married, and she watched her nieces and nephew grow up. Then in 1989 at the age of ninety-four Tante Elizabeth died and was buried in the family boveda.

"Father insisted we put those awful statues in it with her," said Elena. "He claimed she wanted them with her. They are some sort of heirloom. I never heard her say anything about them, and I certainly should have known. I was the only member of the family who paid her the slightest heed."

"You don't like them, then," I said.

James gave me a warning look.

"I hate them. I want Tante to have two beautiful white angels with drooping wings, one on each side of the flower bowl."

"I have an idea," said Alfredo over coffee as he ordered brandy all around.

Miss Elena looked up, interested.

"I happen to know of just such a pair of angels," he said. "I suggest we meet tomorrow at your boveda at, say, eleven o'clock. I'll bring the angels and we can exchange them if you approve of what I bring. The ones I have in mind are beautifully made and I think they would do justice to Tante Elizabeth. No one said the statues she has now had to stay there forever."

Miss Elena's eyes widened as she thought this over. She looked down at James.

"I should love that above all else," she said softly. "Should I do it?"

James looked up soulfully into her eyes and slowly nodded his head.

Miss Elena nodded back. Then with a great sigh, she looked at her watch.

"I must leave now," she said. "I have had a wonderful day and I thank you all, especially this wonderful cat. You wouldn't consider leaving him with me, I suppose. I should be devoted to him."

"I'm sure he would be devoted to you," I said, "but he belongs to a duchess in London who would be devastated if he were not returned."

The captain came to tell us Miss Elena's cab was ready.

"I'll see you tomorrow at eleven in La Recoleta," she said. She stumped off on her short legs, her little grey eyes dancing.

I paid the lunch bill, which was enormous, then Alberto, James and I left to find his car.

"Have you really got two angels?" I asked as we drove back to the center of town.

"Of course," said Alberto. "They are part of a lot of paintings and sculpture we bought outright from an American who is going back to the states after many years. We do that sometimes. Rather than auctioning off these girls, I'll sell them to you at a fair price and you can exchange them for the terra-cotta statues if Miss Elena puts in an appearance tomorrow. They are heavy so I'll bring a handler along and a dolly."

Alberto dropped us off at the hotel, and James and I each took a long nap; we were exhausted. We woke up briefly, ordered soup and salad from room service, watched CNN on television, and fell asleep again and did not waken till the next morning.

Alberto and two helpers arrived on schedule with a small van containing two lumpy objects wrapped in quilts. James and I got in front with Alberto and we were on our way to La Recoleta. Now that I knew what to look for I could see the walls at a distance. Massive brick to a height of about twenty feet. Above the top of the wall poked the tops of angels' wings and the spires of especially elaborate sculptures.

We parked the van, unloaded it and put each lumpy object on

a hand truck. They were not very large, but marble is very heavy. Each young man wheeled an object. James, Alberto and I walked sedately down the main street. Then James could stand it no longer and ran ahead to see if Miss Elena would be there. He returned grinning and we knew she had come. Then he disappeared, and as we turned the now familiar corner there he was, sitting next to Miss Elena, who was standing in front of her boveda dressed in another drab but expensive skirt and jacket. Her little grey eyes were sparkling.

"Good morning, James," she said, patting him on the head. He purred.

"I am so glad you have come," she said to us. "I was afraid you would just think it was all the to-do of a silly old woman."

For just a moment I felt terrible pangs of guilt, but they passed immediately.

"Let's look at what we've brought and see if you like them," Alberto said and motioned to the two young men to remove the quilts.

There in the sunlight were two marble angels, their heads bowed in grief, their wings folded. They were charming, sweet and beautifully executed. The marble was smooth and white.

Miss Elena looked at them for a long time. She felt the smooth cold marble. She looked at the altar inside the glass door.

We all waited.

"They are perfect," she said, and she began to cry. "Tante Elizabeth will love them," she said at last.

Then she took out a handkerchief, blew her nose and wiped her eyes. She took the key out of her handbag and opened the door. She stepped inside and reached over the altar and picked up a terra-cotta and handed it to me. I put it very carefully on the ground. James inspected it carefully and nodded his head. Then she reached over for the other one and we repeated the performance. She stepped out and allowed the young men to lift one angel into position. There were a few changes of angle needed and then the second angel was put in place. Miss Elena stepped back and surveyed the result.

"Will your father be angry?" I asked.

"He never comes here," she laughed. "He isn't even going to be buried here. He is going to be 'laid to rest,' as they say, in his wife's family boveda in the city of Mendosa where the vineyards are."

She closed the door and locked it. We all stood looking at the effect. It was indeed a great deal more traditional. It was also more appropriate. I wrapped the terra-cottas, each in its own quilt, and carefully carried them back to the van.

James and Alberto strolled with Miss Elena.

I returned, leaving the young men to guard the van.

"Can we have a celebratory lunch?" I asked.

"I'm so sorry," said Miss Elena. "I have an appointment at the church to plan a new social program and I absolutely must be there. I hope you understand and I also hope those ugly brown things are adequate compensation for those glorious angels."

"I need only one thing from you, if I may," I asked.

"What is it?"

"Will you write a note saying that these came from your family and that you have exchanged them for two marble sculptures, and sign it?"

She looked thoughtful for a minute, and I thought I had lost the provenance. Then she stopped, sat on a bench at the side of the boulevard under the cypress trees and produced a notebook from her handbag with sheets of paper in it with her name engraved. She wrote out what I had asked with a gold fountain pen. She tore off the sheet, dated it at the bottom and handed it to me.

"Can we take you somewhere?" I asked.

"No, I have my own car here," she said. She didn't get up. Instead she picked up James, who was standing beside her, and hugged him, putting her face next to his.

"I wish I could keep you forever," she whispered in James's ear.

Then she looked at both of us. "You know, because I met this cat and you two and finally did something of my own I've been wanting to do for years, my life has changed." She smiled her nice smile, stood up, relinquishing James, and stomped off on her short legs, turning to wave as she went through the colonnaded entrance to the cemetery.

James and I floated on air all the way back to the hotel. I wrote Alberto a check for the two angels. They were not cheap, but the amount was as nothing compared to what the models would bring someday.

Then we came to earth and called British Airways. Did they have a first-class seat on the plane to London that evening? They did. I reserved it. One problem solved. The next one was harder, but I discovered that if I threw everything out of my soft suitcase it would hold the two models, each wrapped in underwear. I left behind my toilet kit, two books, a good suit and an extra pair of shoes. I would carry the suitcase myself and, on the plane, put it under the seat, not in the overhead bin, so it would not be pushed around.

We arranged to keep the room for the day and, leaving the precious statuettes in the bag in the room, went off to meet Alberto for a farewell luncheon at Las Nazarenas, where we ate *lomo*, the best beef in the world, and drank fine Argentine red wine.

"I wonder why Miss Elena was so adamant about not drinking Argentine wine?" I mused.

"She told us, not in so many words, but you remember her mother comes from a family of Mendosa vintners."

"Of course," I said. "What a strange family."

James was chasing a piece of lomo around his plate.

"Thank you for finding her and working your magic on her," I said, patting him on the head.

He gave me a stern look. He sat as straight as he could. He looked at me with great disapproval. For a moment I was very puzzled. Then I knew what he meant.

"James," I said, abashed, "you are quite right. We broke all the rules. We seduced—well, you seduced—a poor, lonely middle-aged woman. Then we exchanged her very valuable models for a pair of ordinary marble angels."

Alberto was laughing at us both.

"It's a private affair, too complicated to explain, but I owe James an apology."

James nodded his acceptance and then broke into a big grin.

There were some anxious minutes on the trip home, particularly during the long wait in the immigration line at Heathrow, but James was a saint and made not a sound or a move even when a man behind us kept kicking the carry-bag when I set it on the floor beside me.

We sailed through the nothing-to-declare line and were at last safe, home with our prizes. We took a cab to Baron's Chambers where we parted.

"See you tonight?" I asked.

James nodded, winked, and was off to announce his return.

I brooded for all of ten seconds over the conning of Miss Elena. Then I put in a long-distance call to my client, old G. L. He was ecstatic. I gave him the total of all I had spent and he laughed. I asked him if I could have the statuettes photographed at the Huntingdown. He agreed at once. We arranged for insurance on the models while they were in my possession and agreed that as soon as the photographs were taken I would send them the safest, fastest way possible to him in New York. Old G. L. is a big fat man in his sixties, but from the sound of things he was capering around his library with his cordless phone in his hand as though he were a thirty-year-old who had won the million-dollar lottery. Perhaps for him, he had.

My next call was to Costain Cummings.

"This is absolutely paralyzing news," said Costain, when I told him of my find. "I can only gasp when I think of the searching, poking and prying, not to mention the fabrication, that will go on now that it appears Roubiliac made a number of models. I look forward with unalloyed enthusiasm to your imminent appearance here."

"I shall be there in about twenty minutes at the most," I said, and hung up, took my suitcase with the models in it and caught a cab. In less than twenty minutes I was greeting Costain, who was standing at the door of the museum.

In his office I opened the suitcase and removed the precious models. They had survived the trip unmarked. I told him all my adventures, and we both were challenged by the idea that there might be a model for each marble Roubiliac had ever made. Costain signed a receipt for them and called the Photography Department, who sent the department head to pick them up.

Then we walked back through the museum, which was now open to the public. The collection consists mainly of seventeenth- and eighteenth-century objects—paintings, miniatures, sculptures, furniture, glass, porcelain and textiles. There are a few objects from much earlier periods but this part of the collection is not extensive. While the collection is not huge, it is of unusually high quality, and Costain and his staff do a particularly good job of displaying the material. Like most museums, this one has a museum shop with reproductions of some of the objects in the collection. Small sculptures, jewelry, porcelain, and so forth, as well as books on art, postcards, notepaper and all the other usual museum store items.

On our way out I stopped at the store for a moment. "You have unusually good reproductions in this shop," I commented.

"Our Reproduction Department is the envy of museums everywhere," said Costain proudly. "Mr. Samuel Wentworth, head of the department, is unusually skilled."

"Good-bye," I said at the door. "Call me as soon as you are through with the models. My client in New York is eager to get them."

"Indeed, yes," said Costain, "we will move with all speed possible commensurate with accuracy and care."

That afternoon, flat twelve was almost overflowing with friends come by to welcome back the world travellers.

James, his gold earrings glinting, sat on the table. Peter Hightower sat in the big chair. Roger and Poppy sat on the sofa, and Shep and I sat on two of the straight chairs. We were all provided with drinks and a tray of assorted cheeses, a bowl of pretzels for Shep, and a plate of smoked salmon with brown bread. The company had listened to my tale of our adventures. When I explained how we had found Miss Elena and arranged the trade, James sat very still and gave me very disapproving looks.

"You more or less flimflammed the poor old dear, didn't you?" said Poppy.

James nodded. He seemed to have totally ignored his part in the transaction.

"I wouldn't worry, Poppy," said Peter. "Miss Elena has all the money she could ever need and clearly she is a very much happier woman now she has something she thinks appropriate."

"I understand," said Poppy, "I really do. I guess I really feel sorry that she's had such a limited life."

Roger looked at Poppy and his eyes grew soft.

"Now for our news," said Shep, when our story was told. "It has only been three days, but a lot has happened. First, *Cats International* has turned into a huge success, so we are moving it at the end of the month to the Haymarket Theater, and to top it off, Disney Productions has bought the movie rights for a juicy sum of money."

"So here am I, in my first speculation, cleaning up," said Roger happily.

Just then the doorbell sounded. I answered.

"It's Ellen here," said a familiar, reedy voice.

I reported the fact to my guests. Roger, Peter and Shep all shrugged.

"Come on up," I said.

James hissed.

As I went down the hall to open the door, Roger was speaking to James.

"I want to give you a special present," he was saying. "To thank you for making *Cats International* such a success. Without your special direction it would have been just an ordinary musical."

James had assumed his shy, modest look.

As I let Ellen in, Roger had opened a jewel box in which lay a pair of topaz earrings. They exactly matched James's golden eyes.

"Roger," exclaimed Ellen, looking at the earrings. "They're glorious."

Ellen was right—they *were* glorious, and ingenious as well. In addition to a large topaz that hung from a stud, a small circle of topaz stones on a flexible gold chain was so arranged that it could encircle all of James's ear and help support the weight of the large stone.

James yowled. Roger, ignoring Ellen, proceeded to remove a gold earring and install one of the new ones. James shook his head. The earring was secure. He hopped on the back of the chair and looked at himself in the mirror. He beamed. He purred. He jumped onto Roger's lap and licked his face.

Ellen picked up the other one and put it on.

"They are really marvelous, Roger," she said, looking at herself in the mirror.

James stopped licking Roger long enough to hiss at Ellen.

She looked at Roger in surprise. "You aren't going to give these wonderful things to that cat, are you?" she asked.

"I already have," laughed Roger.

Ellen stooped down and before he could properly protest, she had removed James's earring.

"James, dear," she said, "you'd love to lend them to me to wear to the Save the Children ball tomorrow, wouldn't you? Princess Di is going to be there and Harry Kinyata is taking me." She spoke as one speaks to someone totally insignificant to whom it is necessary to be polite.

James sat stunned. So did we all.

Ellen took off the earrings, put them in the box, snapped it shut, put it in her purse, turned and left, letting a "Good-bye all" float over her shoulder as she walked out.

James dashed to the door in a rage but he was too late.

Roger looked very angry. He was speechless.

Shep laughed. "That girl will do anything, won't she?"

"I'll get them back," said Roger.

"What a great bunch we are," said Poppy. "First you and James flimflam an old lady and now this possession-haunted girl comes along and lifts a pair of expensive earrings." Then she smiled. "They really are splendid," she added to Roger. "Did you design them?"

Roger nodded.

"You have talent!" said Poppy, and her eyes were soft.

James was helpless with rage. He knocked the evening paper off the coffee table and proceeded to tear it to pieces. I tried to rescue at least part, as I had not had time to read it, but James only snarled and bared his teeth and slashed with his claws, so I left him alone.

"Want to join us for dinner?" I asked him a little later.

He shook his head and as we went out he walked upstairs, his tail flicking angrily back and forth.

I spent part of the next morning taking stock. The models were at Huntingdown being photographed. They did not need my attention. Two pieces of research were progressing nicely. James was back at work at Thwaites. The topaz earrings were still in Ellen's hands, but I felt sure they would be returned in due time. I decided to stop in at Thwaites to see what was coming up. After looking at what was on show in the great room, I wandered up to the third floor to see Peter.

Marilyn, who usually greets me when I arrive, was standing comforting an older woman who was sitting in the chair Marilyn usually uses, sobbing into an already soaked handkerchief. James was sitting on Marilyn's desk watching intently.

"I wish I knew how to help," said Marilyn to the woman.

"I wish you did too," said the woman between sobs. "It's just that I am frightened all the time and I don't know why. I feel a little safer here." Her sobs subsided somewhat.

"Have you ever thought of seeing a psychiatrist?" Marilyn asked. "I think one might be able to help you."

"I'm afraid to," wailed the woman. At last she got up, blew her red nose and went to wash her face in the lavatory.

Marilyn turned to me. "Poor Elsie," she said. "She is an excellent cataloger but she has been getting more and more unhappy. She is afraid to go out, and it is a terrible struggle for her just to get to the office, and then there is a terrible struggle to go home. She really needs professional care."

James was tugging at me.

"You want to know what a psychiatrist is?" I said.

James nodded.

"A psychiatrist is a doctor who deals with emotional problems such as Elsie's. He helps you unravel the associations that cause your anxiety." While grossly oversimplified, I thought this explanation would do for the moment.

James nodded. Then he squared his shoulders and marched off in search of Elsie. He seemed determined to become a psychiatrist and solve her problems. It would take his mind off his missing earrings.

He found Elsie sitting at her desk looking gloomily into space at nothing. He insinuated himself beside her. Slowly, she let her hand stroke him. He purred gently but did not move. The technique that had been a success with Miss Elena might do here for starters. At last Elsie looked at him.

"Nice kitty," she said.

He purred a little louder and rubbed his face very slowly against her hand. She smiled.

Peter was free so I stopped watching the doctor at work and went into Peter's office.

"James has a new profession," I said. "He's becoming a psychiatrist."

"Good," said Peter. "Shortly we'll all go to lunch with Dr. George Levithan, an excellent psychiatrist who is also a collector. He has just brought in some material for us to sell and I'm taking him to lunch at the club."

At noon James and I joined Peter at his club, where we were introduced to Dr. Levithan. Peter cleverly got the doctor to talk about how he managed some of his cases while James listened so intently he forgot to eat. In fact, at one point he moved to sit on a ledge that was almost directly under Dr. George's hand. Shortly thereafter, the doctor began to stroke James in an abstract sort of way. James purred very softly, and Dr. George stopped talking about cases and told us several very poignant stories from his own youth. When he was finished we were all silent for a moment. Then he stopped stroking James and resumed his professional manner.

After lunch, James and I said good-bye to Peter and Dr. George and headed back to Baron's. James wore his smug expression. The one that says I-know-all-there-is-to-know on a given subject. This time it was psychiatry.

He watched the tenants with a new intensity as they came and went, and in the late afternoon when Roger and Poppy came to call, he sat next to Poppy and listened to her carefully, but first he patted Roger on the ear.

"I know," said Roger ruefully. "I'll get them back, don't worry. I don't want that girl to have them any more than you do."

Poppy was full of excitement. She didn't need James to open her up. She had just been offered what she defined as "the perfect job." A school in Amsterdam had commissioned her to design costumes for a special pageant. The school had little money, so the costumes had to be made of inexpensive materials and had to be easy enough to make so that unskilled students could make them. The pageant itself had to do with nature—something to do with emphasizing environmental protection.

"You see," said Poppy, "it has all the elements I love—children, a technical challenge, an emphasis on nature and, I might add, a most agreeable group of adults to work with. I'll be gone about two weeks, maybe. Of course, it barely pays expenses, but who minds that."

"But what about me?" asked Roger wistfully.

"Come along," said Poppy.

"Can't," said Roger. "I have to stay and pay attention to my investments. Besides, I have money in a new show."

"You and your money!" said Poppy with some asperity. For some reason Poppy hates the idea of wealth.

At last we all went out to Wheeler's for a fish dinner.

As we were leaving the restaurant to go our separate ways, James flipped his ears back and forth.

"I know," said Roger, "I know."

The next day James spent the morning at Thwaites. Peter watched him and reported that James approached Elsie as he had before and just sat under her hand. At first she stroked him, then she began to talk to him in a very faint whisper. James could not hear exactly what she said, but he stayed perfectly still and purred gently. She was not crying, and when Jerry, whose job it was to distribute the mail, memos and messages, bounced in to deliver her mail, she did not jump with fright. At noon Elsie sat at her desk eating lunch. As usual she refused to go out with any of the others.

James returned to Baron's for the afternoon, found me going out and patted his ear.

"I'll call Roger," I said, "but tonight is his opening, so we won't see him and I have to go to a society meeting, so you won't see me, but check tomorrow." James waved in salute.

The following day he repeated the procedure with Elsie but something unusual happened. Elsie almost immediately picked James up and carried him into the women's lounge, where she sat in a comfortable chair and cried, talked, and cried some more, soaking James's head in the process. Because he has great self-control when he needs it, he kept on purring, despite the fact that Elsie's dismal tale, which he could now understand, was not at all interesting. At last she dried up, washed her face and returned to the office, carrying James on her ample hip. Then she did something she had never done before. She went up to Marilyn, who was sitting at the front desk.

"May I go to lunch with you?" she said, blushing. "I'll pay my way and I won't talk much."

Marilyn smiled. "What a good idea," she said. "But you'd better put James down. He can't come with us."

"Oh, yes," said Elsie, blushing even harder. "Sorry, James."

James rubbed against her leg once he was released and tastefully waited till Elsie and Marilyn had gone before returning to Baron's.

He scratched at my door about five o'clock as I was reading the *Financial Times*. I put the paper on the table and opened the door for him, and at that moment the bell rang. I spoke into the intercom.

"It's Ellen," came a breathy voice.

"It's Ellen," I told James as I hung up the phone. "She's coming up."

She always seemed to turn up when Roger was expected. He and Shep were due shortly.

I let her in. She opened her purse, took a jeweler's box out and walked over to the table where James was reclining next to the paper.

"Here are the earrings," she said, looking at the paper. Then she stiffened. She tried to pick up the box again, but a paw with claws extended caught her hand.

"Ouch," she said, sucking her little finger.

James was up and sitting on the table, the earring box under his paws and the paper all over the floor.

Roger and Shep took that moment to arrive.

"Sorry about the play," Shep was saying as they entered. "I guess you really took a bath."

"Lost it all," said Roger, though he did not sound really stricken.

"Hello, Ellen," said Shep.

"I see you brought back the earrings," said Roger. "Thanks."

Ellen was staring at Roger and there was nothing in her eyes but scorn. "To think I wasted my time on you!" she said, "and I got nothing for my efforts except a scratch from that damned cat." She grabbed her purse and slammed out of the apartment on her gorgeous long legs.

James grinned his most evil grin and hurled himself at Shep, who was stretched out in the big chair.

"Watch it, boy," said Shep, and then he and James roughed each other up happily.

"I don't understand," said Roger. "She comes apart just because she learned I lost some money on a play. I told her once how much I was putting into it and it was nothing of importance."

James stopped playing, hopped off Shep's lap and dragged the *Times* out on the floor. He looked at the page carefully and then to our surprise arranged himself on the paper, after a few false starts.

"That's the way he was on the table when Ellen came in," I exclaimed.

Then we all examined the paper.

There was a headline, which read in its entirety:

R. HAMFORD FILES FOR BANKRUPTCY

However, with James's tail in place it read:

R. HAM
BANKRUPTCY

The subhead read:

R. H. Enterprises
To Be Dissolved By Court

Shep howled. Roger laughed ruefully. "I guess she believed it. After all I am always wanting to go to pubs and take the tube and she always wanted the most elaborate restaurants and taxis, so that quick look combined with my comments about the play convinced her."

"You never thought that girl was anything but a cash chaser, did you?" said Shep.

"To tell you the truth I never thought much about her. She is very pretty and she can be flattering, and when I first met her she was fun to play around with. Then I met Poppy and forgot all about her except for the business of the earrings."

In the end we all went out to the nearest pub to celebrate Roger's initiation into losing money in the theater. We had shepherd's pie and James consented to drink stout, about four ounces out of Shep's first pint.

"James," I said sternly as we were riding up to the fourth floor in the elevator. "Do you realize you lied to Ellen?"

James, who was riding on my shoulder so he could push the floor button, patted my mouth. He was looking disgusted. He shook his head. Then we both began to laugh and as I opened the elevator doors, he streaked upstairs, his tail flicking happily back and forth.

James was now a cat of affairs. He spent his mornings at Thwaites performing as a psychiatrist or as a stamp sorter, depending on what was required. The afternoons he spent at Baron's, either sitting on his table checking on tenants or following María around to see that the building was being properly maintained. Peter reported that Elsie was still lugging James into the women's lounge and sobbing on him, but it appeared that as a result, she was less afraid and had taken to going out to lunch frequently. Marilyn reported that Elsie had even been known to laugh. She certainly was working more efficiently.

Fortunately I had nearly completed tracking a painting through a number of sales catalogs to establish its provenance beyond doubt. At the same time I was growing nervous. I had called Costain Cummings three times and each time I was told he was unavailable. Had something happened to the models? The thought left me consumed with anxiety.

Flat twelve was a busy place of a late afternoon. Peter Hightower came by. He sat in the big chair, a glass of La Iña beside him and a plate of salmon with fresh dill and brown bread ready at hand. James, who had sipped some sherry for a change, was sitting happily on his lap. As I looked at my two good friends, the round, pink-cheeked face with its blue eyes smiling happily above the grey furry face with its golden eyes, also smiling happily, I felt for the moment completely happy.

Peter stroked James softly. "You know," he said in his soft

baritone, "you really might be a psychiatrist. I think I'll call you Dr. James. You have been very helpful to Elsie."

James smirked slightly. He knew he was one of the great psychiatrists of the world.

"Elsie came to me right after lunch today," he went on. "She said she wants to see a psychiatrist and would I recommend one and arrange her schedule to fit."

James sat up, surprised. After all, he was a psychiatrist. Why would she need anyone else?

"I had been hoping for a long time we could get her to want to see somebody. It is useless to insist someone see a therapist until there is a desire on the part of the patient."

James patted Peter sharply.

Peter looked down at his friend.

"Now, Doctor," he said. "Don't you think it is better to let her cry in Dr. George's consulting room rather than all over you in the women's lounge?"

James shook his head.

"Come now," Peter continued. "After all, you got her started, which is the important part. The rest sometimes takes years and years."

James's golden eyes flew open in astonishment.

"Psychiatric treatment often takes a long time, and I think a cat with your varied abilities has too much to offer to even consider spending the next two years listening to Elsie sob."

James began to settle back. He half closed his eyes and assumed the air of the Renaissance cat ready for any challenge.

Later on Roger and Lord Henry stopped in, joined us for a sherry, reported all well with Helena and no word from Poppy. We all went off to an early dinner at Colombino's, where James ate ravioli and a wonderful dessert made with fresh cherries, white wine and Drambuie. Over dessert, Roger, who had drunk his share of good red wine, began to talk about himself. I don't suppose the fact that James was sitting right next to him purring softly had anything to do with it, but Roger, who has a fine intelligence and a well-developed sense of humor, almost never talks about himself.

"I don't know what to do about Poppy," he said. He mashed a bread stick into crumbs. "I'm crazy about her. I've never felt like this with any other girl. I think she likes me and we certainly have a wonderful time together, sort of the way you and Helena do."

Lord Henry smiled. "Then ask her to marry you," he said.

"I have," said Roger, "a number of times. She says she can't give up her independence."

"What does she mean by that?" said Peter. "You haven't threatened to lock her up, have you?"

"No," Roger laughed. "She says that I have all this money, which I do, and that if she marries me she will have to give up her career because no one will take her seriously anymore. Like Helena, she says. She wants to make her mark in her profession, not be the rich wife of a successful investor and besides, she says, money is immoral." Roger sighed.

"Well," said Peter, "why don't you just live together, sometimes at her place and sometimes at yours?"

James looked up from his plate of dessert and glared at Peter. James believes in marriage and family.

"What would we do with the children, move them about?" asked Roger, laughing.

Lord Henry smiled. "So you want children. What about Poppy, does she want children, too?"

"She loves kids and sometimes the thought of a family of her own is just right, and then she says we will be overpopulating and ruining the environment and she will have to leave them to a nanny if she is to go on with her work, and besides it is sinful to bring children into a world of atom bombs and constant wars. I just don't know what she wants. I only know I miss her terribly when she's gone."

Roger looked very unhappy at that moment. Then he recovered his usual even disposition. We talked for a bit longer and then separated for home.

The next morning I finally got through to Costain Cummings.

"Where have you been?" I asked.

"Terribly involved," he said. "I suppose you are looking for your models."

"Yes, you must be through with them by now." I sounded a little sharp.

"I have been after them," said Costain, "and Photography assures me they will be back in my office tomorrow morning. Will you put in an appearance?"

"I'll be there at nine o'clock," I said.

"Excellent," said Costain and rang off.

I went about my business. James went about his. Since I fully expected to pick up the models the next day, I stopped off at Thwaites's shipping department, where the supervisor knows me well, and arranged to have the two pieces packed and shipped by air, special valuable merchandise handling. I heaved a silent sigh of relief. That assignment was almost finished.

That evening James came by and had only finished his usual survey of the apartment, which he makes every time he comes, when the bell rang and visitors were at hand. Poppy arrived, back from Amsterdam with an elegant Edam cheese. Roger brought a single-malt whiskey from Islay called Lagavulin, which we had never tasted. Shep came with some Guinness stout and Jane Jensen carried a big briefcase along with herself.

I put the contributions away and took orders, and James seated the guests, making sure that Poppy and Roger were next to each other on the sofa and that Shep had the big chair, so he could stretch his long legs and James could jump on him. Jane and I had to be content with straight chairs.

"You call it "La-ga-*voo*-lin," said Roger. "The distillery where it comes from is right next door to the Laphroaig distillery on the island of Islay in the Hebrides."

Roger, James, Poppy, Jane and I tasted. Shep slurped stout.

James tasted once more, considered, tasted again, smiled, tasted again and fell over grinning.

"I guess he likes it," I said, "and so do I."

James took a brief nap, during which he missed most of Poppy's account of her trip to Amsterdam, which had been, from her point of view, hugely successful. Her simple patterns for costumes had been easy for the children to follow and had inspired some excellent variations. The pageant had been enthusiastically received by a much larger audience than expected, and the performance itself had been very moving and impressive-looking. Of course, the management had not been able to pay her a fee at all but did pay her expenses. Poppy regarded it as a huge success and talked about next year.

I was glad James did not hear all this as he is a stout capitalist at heart and would not have approved.

"Roger certainly should have seen it," said Jane. "I was in Amsterdam when it went on and the comments in the papers afterward were glowing, particularly about how visually exciting it was. 'Poppy Balsom is a great new talent,' they said."

"Oh, come," said Poppy, blushing. Her account had not included any mention of this praise.

"I'll be there next time, wherever it is," said Roger.

"Don't hold your breath," said Shep. "He'll be involved in some investment that requires all his time and won't leave his office in the city."

James, now fully alert, jumped off the coffee table onto Shep's lap with claws extended.

"Ouch," Shep howled, "that hurt." James gave him a sharp look and hopped back to the table for another little taste.

Jane now abruptly changed the subject. Turning to Shep she said, "I'm delighted to meet you. I came especially because Roger said you'd be here. I have a proposition for you."

"I love being propositioned," said Shep.

James yowled.

"I am a public relations expert," said Jane in a matter-of-fact voice. "I have an office on Fleet Street and quite a thriving business. You directed and produced *Puss-in-Boots* last year. It was very effective. I need someone to produce a cat feature for me so I came to you."

"I did *Puss-in-Boots*," said Shep, "but it was James who really made it such a success."

James stood up on Shep's lap, teetered on his hind leg, waved his paw and collapsed.

"I want to do a documentary on cats in London. The Humane

Society will use it for a care-for-your-cat drive. They want a fifteen-minute film. Another group wants a number of different stills. The pay is excellent. Do you know of anyone who would do such a job?"

Shep looked at James. James looked at Shep.

"Want to appear on TV again?" Shep asked.

James nodded, hopped off Shep's lap for the coffee table, where he took another sip of Lagavulin and hopped back. He was just the least bit unsteady.

"I'd like to do it, myself," said Shep.

"Excellent," said Jane. She took a diary out of her purse. "When?"

"As soon as possible," Shep answered. "My next project is waiting for a team of writers to agree and that will take some time. Meantime I'll get a sound man and a cameraman who can do both stills and film. It shouldn't take long. We'll take James along for luck. Well, really more than luck. If we can't find any city cats, he's a very versatile performer."

James nodded, turned on his back and applauded himself by patting his paws together while Shep scratched his tummy.

"Fine," said Jane. She picked up her large briefcase, put it on the table and opened it, revealing a personal computer complete with roll of paper. I showed her where to plug it in and she rapidly typed out a contract, which she handed to Shep. While he was reading his, she typed another for James.

"Is James your cat?" she asked me.

I explained that James belonged to Mrs. March who lived on the next floor up, and before I could add any details Jane had dashed off, her high-heeled patent leather pumps flashing as she ran up the stairs. Jane is a very well put-together girl from her sleek black hair through the always crisp tailored dresses she wears to her patent leather pumps.

115

She returned shortly with a signed contract for the use of James in a documentary and for still shots. While she was gone, Shep had called his favorite cameraman and found him available.

Business completed, Jane smiled at us all, folded up her computer, said good-bye and ran down the stairs.

"I'll call with dates," she said over her shoulder as she circled the elevator shaft. Jane never uses the lift.

I looked at James and decided it was time for dinner. Poppy and Roger were going to try a new vegetarian restaurant. James quietly shook his head when they asked us if we wanted to join them. Shep went off to have dinner with his cameraman, and James and I went to Frank's nearby and had a bowl of soup. James had a cassata and we came home to watch the news on TV. James patted the bottle of Lagavulin in passing.

"Good stuff?" I asked.

He nodded, closed his eyes and "watched" the news that way. It is easier for him to concentrate. When Mrs. March knocked, you might almost say he woke with a start, looked around and then left to walk upstairs with great dignity. He wobbled a little though.

The next morning I found James sitting on his table. I had the carry-bag in my hand.

"Want to go to the Huntingdown and pick up the models?" I asked.

James grinned, hopped off the table and into the bag, which I held for him. Then we were off in a cab. After all, my client was paying for it.

The guard recognized me and let me in. He did not examine the carry-bag, but James stayed in it till we reached Costain Cumming's office.

"Enter," called Costain.

I went in. James did not follow so I left the door open.

Costain was sitting at his desk, an abstracted expression on his face. There were no statues to be seen.

"This is very strange indeed," said Costain. "I spoke to Photography only last night, and they assured me the statues would be here this morning. It is possible their definition of 'first thing' does not coincide with mine, but I am deeply concerned."

"I am even more so," I said gloomily.

James appeared at the door, yowled and beckoned to us to follow him. Costain was not impressed but I was, so I moved as fast as I could to follow James down a corridor into a large workroom where there was a battered desk that held one of my statues. On the floor beside the desk was a large wooden crate filled with packing material. James ran straight to the desk, took one look at the statue and knocked it to the floor.

"James," I gasped, "have you lost your mind?"

It was only then that I noticed a bald, fat man in a laboratory coat, standing to one side of the desk, glaring at James, who was now trying to uncover something in the crate.

"Scat!" cried the man.

James paid no attention. By this time Costain had arrived.

"Sam," he said, "what is all the commotion for?"

"This cat came charging in here and knocked your statue off the desk. He seems to have broken the top in the process."

Sure enough, Handel was headless. The head had rolled under the desk.

James was systematically uncovering another terra-cotta model in the crate.

He stopped long enough to leap out of the crate and point to the statue of Handel lying headless on the floor. He patted the base and shook his head. I picked up the headless statue and looked carefully at the base. There was no monogram. In fact, as I looked very carefully at the piece, I realized that it was a reproduction. An excellent one, but certainly a reproduction.

"Where are the originals?" I demanded.

James jumped back in the crate. I nodded to him and he moved away so I could pull out the one he had exposed.

There in my hands was George Friedrich himself complete with monogram on the base.

"And the other one?" I asked.

James pointed to the crate. The bald man stood apparently stunned. Costain was, for the moment, speechless.

I uncovered a second statue in the crate and placed it with the first one. James and I checked it over. We did indeed have the originals. I looked around and on a shelf behind the desk I found the other copy.

"Please, return to my office and I will join you in just a moment," said Costain in a strange voice.

I carried the statues, one in each hand, and James preceded me to the curator's office, where I sank into a chair.

James sat on the desk and looked very worried. His ears twitched. We waited for about ten minutes. Costain returned.

"I am so sorry. It is all a terrible misunderstanding," he said.

James shook his head.

"Photography got mixed up and sent the statues to the work-rooms with a slip asking that they be reproduced for the store.

Sam was about to send them back to Photography when we happened along."

James shook his head.

"In a wooden crate?" I asked.

"No, no, the one we found on the desk was to go back to Photography. Sam had just made a terrible mistake. He is beside himself with mortification. He just made a mistake."

James shook his head.

"What is it, James?" I asked.

"Did he make a mistake?"

James shook his head.

"Do you know for sure?"

A nod. "How?" James looked around for a minute, then patted the telephone on Costain's desk. "You heard him talking on the phone to someone?" James nodded and smiled. "He was arranging to send the originals to someone?" I made a wild guess. James nodded. "Who?" James shook his head. He didn't know. "Did he see you?" James seemed unsure. I interpreted "maybe."

Costain Cummings was looking at two pieces of paper on his desk which he had brought with him. He passed one to me. It was a museum form authorizing the transfer of a piece of work from one department to another. There was a space for a description of the object and a space for date and time and, at the bottom, a signature. This form had "Photography" filled in at the top. "Reproduction" was indicated as the destination and the words "two terra-cotta statues" were written in the space for description. The paper was dated a week ago at 5:00 P.M. and signed with an undecipherable scrawl.

"Does the name mean anything to you?" I asked.

"It could be anybody," Costain said. He looked very unhappy.

He picked up his phone and asked the store to send packing materials. When a young girl arrived with a carton box and tissue paper, we packed the terra-cottas safely for transport to Thwaites.

Costain patted James. "A profound obeisance I make to you, sir," he said to James, who looked confused. "Without your perspicacity we would have lost all. This is not the end of this business. Wentworth's obfuscations will not stand."

I thanked him and hurried out with James, back in the carry-bag with a puzzled expression on his face, and the carton box in my arms. We got a cab immediately and went directly to Thwaites, where I turned the precious pieces over to the shipping department with a deep sigh.

At last I turned to James. "He meant he made you a big bow and that without your clever brains we would all have been in deep soup and that the bald man is going to be in for trouble."

James grinned and capered around the shipping room tossing little pieces of wiggly Styrofoam packing material in the air. Then he went off to see where he was needed on the third floor, and I went back to Baron's to call G. L. and report that, at last, the statues were on their way.

By six that evening James and I had calmed down somewhat and were ready to take on a new adventure. I wondered a bit about what Costain Cummings would do about Mr. Wentworth, but I was mistakenly certain that it was not my problem.

James was in the sitting room when the bell rang and Shep

announced that he, Jane and a van were waiting below. Inside the van we found Jane in blue jeans and a shirt. She carried a clipboard with a pencil attached and made notes as we went along. A cameraman, a sound man and all their equipment were also installed. There was barely room for me, and James sat on my lap.

Though it was six-thirty, the sun was still shining brightly and the grass, trees and flowers all had a lovely golden sheen. Green Park was our first stop. We parked the van on the street near the Stafford Hotel and walked into the park through a passage between two apartment houses. For a while we sat on the grass and waited for a cat to appear. However, park cats are not curious about people and James began to get bored. He left us and began to explore the gardens and hedges on the edge of the park. He flushed a cat and chased it. The cat made for a big tree and started up. Tor, our cameraman, who had consented to do both film and stills, was up and running. He is a lean young Finn whose hobby, when he isn't taking pictures, is marathon running. Our sound man, Moises, originally from Spain, sat where he was. Sound could be dubbed in on these pictures, if we got any.

Tor and James began to work together. Tor said in his normal voice, "James, can you move the cat to the other side of the tree? The light is much better."

James chased the cat around the tree to a better position.

"Good," said Tor. "Now back off and pretend you are not interested and perhaps the cat will come down."

James wandered away, apparently bored, and the cat, after a few minutes, came slowly down the tree. It was a very scruffy small calico. Tor got an excellent close-up of the cat in the grass.

"Come up very slowly," said Tor. "I want to see if I can get him to defend himself."

James approached slowly. The calico cat arched its back, bared its teeth and snarled.

So now we had a method. Once Moises saw what was happening, he placed himself where he could pick up the appropriate sounds of the animals. We flushed another cat in Green Park. Back at the van, where we had left Shep in charge of all our equipment, we reported on our success.

"Great," he said, ruffling James's fur. "You flush 'em and herd 'em, we'll take 'em."

We explored St. James's churchyard. We found a cat on Trafalgar Square eating a pigeon. We found a number on the embankment. By nine we had a lot of good film.

As I watched James work, I realized how little contact he had had with other cats in his life. He was a successful herder, but he was startled and frightened when a strange cat started spitting at him. He was larger than most of the cats we found and certainly in much better condition, but he was very tentative. If I didn't know that James had courage along with every other virtue, I'd say he was afraid.

Back at flat twelve with a saucer of Lagavulin, which he now preferred to Laphroaig, James was an expansive member, not to say star, of the film crew. After a quick drink and a certain amount of washing up, we all repaired to Frank's for a late supper.

Back at the flat, we sat together, James on my lap, to watch the late, late news.

"Thanks for finding the statues," I said softly.

There was a knock at the door. James did not move. I got up, carrying him carefully, opened the door and handed him, still sound asleep, to Mrs. March.

"He's had a long, hard day," I said.

She snuggled him in her arms. "Doesn't let you do this often, does he?" she said as she carried him off to bed.

The next morning James spent sitting on his table inspecting tenants. About eleven he slipped into Thwaites and listened while Elsie talked to him. She no longer cried all the time, but now she was sometimes very cross with him. At noon she left to go to lunch with Marilyn and two other members of her staff. James peered into Peter's office. There was Dr. George, just settling into the visitor's chair. Peter waved at James.

"Come in, come in," he called, and patted his lap.

James accepted the invitation and curled up on his old friend's ample lap.

"What do you think of my collection?" asked Dr. George. "Is it worth auctioning?"

"I'll let you see the lotting in about a week, but I think it will do very well in our nineteenth-century European sale in Zurich sometime in August."

"I'm delighted," said Dr. George, "and by the way, thanks for making things easy for Elsie. She told me to tell you, so I'm not breaking any confidences. We are getting along very well. It's almost as though someone had done all the preliminary work. She keeps talking about some magic cat. We'll get to the bottom of that before long, I'm sure." Then he bounced out of his chair and, with a wave of his hand and a cheery good-bye he was out the door and gone.

Peter and James looked at each other and both burst out laughing. Peter made his chair go up and down, and then they went together to the East India Club, where they had lunch and a long nap in Peter's room.

It was about five-thirty when James scratched at my door just as the phone rang. I let him in and answered.

"The models are safe and sound, and they are better than I expected. I will deposit your fee plus a substantial bonus in your account. You can wait till you get the deposit slip to find out the amount. Now find Florence Nightingale," said old G. L. in one breath, and without waiting for an answer he hung up.

Florence Nightingale is another of Roubiliac's sculptures in Westminster Abbey.

"They're safe in the hands of old G. L.," I told James, and we frolicked around the living room until the bell rang announcing the filming crew. We hurried downstairs and climbed in the van.

We parked in an area where we could find a number of street markets. There were plenty of scrawny cats around the food stalls, and while I became a customer, James flushed a number of them. There is almost no light under a stall and the cats are not out in the open on top of the merchandise, so after a few good shots taken with great effort we decided to leave the market streets. However, we were able to film one excellent sequence involving a grey tiger-striped cat playing with a dead mouse. The stall owner hated all the cats that were underfoot, and when he heard we were doing a documentary on London's street cats, he let us in his stall with lights and even provided the dead mouse as a lure.

James watched the whole performance with great apprehension.

"That cat will eat that mouse before long," I said to James as we watched. James shuddered.

In an alley as we left the market, James found a mother cat with three new kittens. She was nested in the corner of an abandoned garage and we needed our lights. James was fascinated by the kittens and trotted over to look at them. The mother cat arched her back and snarled. James, startled, jumped back, looked around and came to sit next to me. Tor got some excellent pictures of the kittens and was bubbling.

Jane was noting each shot on the clipboard, recording the subject, length of time filmed and any relevant details. She made no comment, but Shep was delighted. After he left us at the end of a session, he and Tor reviewed the film we had taken.

"James," he said at one point, "this is going to be a really splendid piece, thanks to you."

James only nodded. He wanted to get home and groom himself. James is not one for the rough life.

Tor was not ready to go home, however. Instead, he had made a purchase at the fish market and now directed Shep to head for the warehouses around the customs house near the Tower. James gave me a grim look but we were off.

I now became a member of the team because it was getting late and the light was fading. At last we found what Tor wanted. An open area in the midst of warehouses near the river. Shep and I carried the battery-driven lights, and James trotted along beside me looking uneasily about him. Tor took a flounder out of the package he had bought at the fishmonger and placed it in the middle of an open space. Then we all moved back against a wall and waited as quietly as possible. No lights, no sound except, eventually, the meowing of cats as they carefully approached the flounder.

"Now," said Tor.

I turned on my light, Shep turned on his. In the center of the open space were three cats all tearing at the fish and snarling at one another. James looked around in terror and jumped onto Jane's lap on top of her clipboard. He does not know Jane well and usually ignores her, but she was the only safe spot. Shep, Tor, Moises and I were all standing with our hands full.

After a moment, the cats ignored the lights and put on a fine show of fighting over a fish. Tor and Moises got the whole splendid cat fight. James closed his eyes for that.

At last we had had enough and returned to the van.

"That's all we need of wild cats." said Jane as we drove home.

James and I were both too tired to go out so we shared a bowl of canned clam chowder and a little milk, and he tottered up to bed, stunned and exhausted by the night's work.

The next day Jane called, and I made an appointment to meet her at a studio that evening to see the film we had shot. I picked up James and we took a cab because I was currently rich, and before long we were sitting in a studio looking at a big television screen while Tor ran film for us. Shep and Moises sat beside us. We were all critics now. I thought Tor had done an outstanding job, but the subjects James had gotten for us were also excellent and all of us were euphoric at the end of the presentation.

Everyone started talking at the same time, offering suggestions and exclaiming over particularly good shots. James was bored. He started tossing a cassette he found on a table back and forth.

"What's that?" I asked.

Tor looked at it, slipped it into the VCR and started it.

It turned out to be a video Tor had shot during the dress rehearsal of *Cats International*. First we saw Ursula warming up, then James demonstrating some movements, then Ursula imitating. Ursula smiled at James. He did a somersault. Then we switched to Poppy Balsom making up Anne. The segment concluded with a shot of the finale.

"That's it. That's our lead-in," said Jane. "Thanks, James."

He gave her his think-nothing-of-it look.

There remained only the still pictures to be taken, so Jane and Tor appeared the next afternoon without Shep. We would take the pictures in flat twelve. James had slept well but he was still somewhat tired and certainly bored with performing for the camera. And while Tor shot some film, he was not really satisfied. Then the bell rang and Helena and Poppy were there. I welcomed them with open arms.

James was now changed with charm. His favorite artist in the whole world had arrived. James liked Poppy, too, so he began to behave like a proper host, and Tor took some pictures of him as he greeted his friends and was patted in return. Then, while I fixed iced tea for the ladies, James showed off. He sat, crouched, pounced, stalked, stretched, played with a ball of paper, waved a paw, smirked, winked and glowered. At last he launched himself from the high windowsill to the floor with a wild yowl. Tor was lying on the floor by this time shooting picture after picture. Helena and Poppy laughed and applauded. At last

James collapsed, exhausted. Jane put away her pencil. Tor packed up his cameras, and the publicist and photographer departed with good wishes all around, and Helena, Poppy, James and I were left in peace.

Helena stretched out on the sofa, iced tea at hand. Poppy was curled up comfortably in the big chair and James lay negligently on the arm, just under Poppy's hand. She stroked him gently; he purred. The psychiatrist was at work.

"I keep thinking about Roger," mused Poppy, almost to herself. "I like him too much"—deep sigh—"in fact, I think I love him." More vigorous stroking. "In fact I'm sure I love him"—deep sigh—"but I'm afraid to marry him. He has all that beastly money. If I marry him, I'll lose all my professional identity, and besides, I'll have to do all those rich things like have servants to run my big house and live a kind of life I disapprove of." James purred softly.

There was a small, comfortable silence.

Poppy turned to Helena. "You were a struggling artist when you married Henry. Now you're a rich Lady Haverstock with a huge house and Wilson and all those people to run it. What has happened to your work? You could get any gallery in town to hang your work just because you're Lady Haverstock. It wouldn't have to be any good."

Helena was silent for a moment, thinking.

"Of course, you could go on painting; in fact, I know you do. But suppose you had a career that took you out of the house. You would have to go where the job took you. I have been offered a job in Oslo later this summer. In fact a lot of my work takes me away. How would Roger like that if we were married?"—deep sigh—"He'd just say 'Why do you rush off all the time when you don't need to? We have plenty of money.'"

James slid out from under Poppy's hand and hopped into her lap. He shook his head and gave her a very disappointed look.

"A lot you know." she said, and dumped him unceremoniously on the floor.

Helena sat up. "It's true," she said, "that some galleries that would never accept my work now take it because I am Lady Haverstock, but it is also true that I can do better work because I do not have to spend my time cleaning other people's houses in order to support my painting. It's a trade-off."

"Well," said Poppy self-consciously, "I really didn't mean to bend your ear." She sounded a bit petulant, but I guessed she was really struggling with herself.

"You are my best friend," said Helena. "I care about everything that concerns you. You could never bend my ear." Then she looked at her watch and determined it was time to go. Poppy picked up her purse and patted James affectionately. "Let's take a cab together," she said.

"Good-bye, Dr. James, sir," said Helena with great affection. James smiled and gave her his paw which she shook ceremoniously.

When I returned from seeing them out, I found James pacing the floor.

"Something bothering you?" I asked.

He nodded.

"You let Poppy know you didn't like what she said about Roger," I guessed.

James nodded again.

"The doctor is not supposed to make any value judgments, is that it?"

James nodded again—short, sharp nods.

"James," I said, "you do a wonderful job. You really can't expect to be perfect."

James gave me a scathing look and we went to dinner, where I was permitted to order anything but flounder.

For a brief time the days of summer lazed along. James had gone back to stamps at Thwaites as Elsie was now going to Dr. George instead of Dr. James. The photography was finished to the satisfaction of everyone. Poppy was off on an assignment and a lonely Roger stopped in from time to time, as did Lord Henry and Helena when they were in town for their natural childbirth sessions. James and I enjoyed the peace. We walked in St. James's Park in the evening and fed the waterfowl. Sometimes we listened to the band concert. Sometimes we would have lunch in Crown Passage and then watch the tourists taking pictures of the guards at St. James's Palace. James looked at St. James's Palace with longing. He really thinks of it as home.

Then, one late afternoon, Mrs. March called to announce that a lawyer, a Mr. Graves, was in her office. He wished to talk to me.

"Send him right down," I said. "I wonder what's up?" I asked James, who was rearranging the ashtray and three pens that were sitting on the table. He nodded absently and brushed a pen off the table. I bent down, picked it up and put it back. He swept another off with his tail and looked at me appealingly. I picked that up. The ashtray, fortunately empty, bumped onto the carpet. James, all surprise, looked over the edge of the table and then up at me, his eyes wide with wonder.

"Bored, aren't you," I said with some asperity. I retrieved the ashtray and put it on the coffee table. I scooped up the pens and put them in the top drawer of the dresser. James hopped over to the windowsill and looked gloomily out into the street. There was a knock at the door. I opened it to admit a plumpish man in a well-cut, dark grey suit. He had carefully combed grey hair, pale blue eyes and a slight double chin. He carried a polished leather briefcase in one hand and a bowler hat in the other.

"How do you do?" he said. "My name is Hudderstone Graves, and I am a solicitor involved in the prosecution of Samuel Wentworth. May I see you for a few minutes?"

"The man at the Huntingdown who tried to steal our statues," I said to James as I waved our guest into the big chair. James left the window and lay flat on the table, looking at Mr. Graves, who now opened his briefcase and removed a yellow legal pad and a gold pen. I offered refreshment. Mr. Graves refused.

"In this case I represent the Crown. Samuel Wentworth is being prosecuted for criminal fraud in connection with a number of objects stolen from the Huntingdown Museum over a considerable period of time. I understand you were involved with one of these thefts."

I told Mr. Graves how I had taken the statues to the Huntingdown for photography and only recovered the originals by a lucky chance and the alert perceptions of my friend, James.

"And where is this friend to be found?" asked Mr. Graves, continuing to write.

"Right here," I answered.

He looked up in surprise.

"James, meet Mr. Graves." I waved my hand. James sat up and extended a paw.

Mr. Graves looked from James to me and back again. He was more than astonished. He was closer to appalled.

"This is not a frivolous business," he said sternly.

"I am not being frivolous. James was indeed there and did find my statues for me."

"You mean you took your cat to the Huntingdown Museum?"

"Indeed I did. Ask Costain Cummings, he will tell you. James has a very good eye; he can often detect forgeries that it takes other experts weeks to uncover." I gave James a serious, professional nod. I was going to mention that James regularly acted in a professional capacity at Thwaites, but I stopped. William Young, Thwaites's managing director would be deeply mortified to have anyone think his auction house employed a cat.

Mr. Graves looked at me with deep suspicion.

"Call Costain and ask him," I said.

Mr. Graves gulped and nodded. I dialed and, finding Costain at home, handed the phone to Mr. Graves.

During the conversation James and I smirked at each other.

Mr. Graves nodded a lot. Costain talks a lot. At last he hung up the phone.

"I can't believe it, but Costain Cummings is too concerned about this business to play a silly practical joke, so I must accept that this cat played a part in the affair," he said, and picked up his gold pen again.

"Let us get the details," he said.

Getting the details was not easy since James could not tell us directly. It went something like this.

"We went to the Huntingdown together," I said.

James nodded.

"You left me and went directly to the reproduction workroom because the door was open and you could see in."

James nodded.

"Could you see the statue on the desk?"

And so on. Finally, Mr. Graves was satisfied with James's story. In fact he was jubilant.

"This is most welcome testimony," he said. "It appears that Mr. Wentworth has been stealing original pieces sent to his workshop for reproduction on a regular basis for some time, but there is no direct evidence to counter his defense that he made a mistake, or someone in his shop made a mistake, and returned reproductions rather than originals to their places in the museum. Here, at last, is direct evidence that Wentworth himself was involved in the theft. The problem will be how to get him to admit it. However, that will be the barrister's problem. I should like to call tomorrow morning to make an appointment for you and, ah, James with Sir A. Grant Paine, our barrister."

"That suit you?" I asked James. He nodded, walked daintily across the table and extended a paw to Mr. Graves, who took it uneasily, then placed his pad and pen in the briefcase and closed it. I handed him his hat and he departed.

"James strikes again," I said.

James rolled off the table. He loves to do that because I am always sure he is going to hurt himself, and so I reach to catch him, he nimbly eludes me and lands safe and sound on his feet. I should learn. He was purring happily.

The night after an early dinner of osso buco at Frank's, James and I played question and answer until I had a complete account of what Samuel Wentworth had said and done before Costain and I arrived in the room. It took a long time but neither of us wanted to stop, and by the time Mrs. March came by, I knew exactly what had happened.

"James here?" she asked.

He nodded to her and walked upstairs with all the dignity befitting a very important witness.

Mr. Graves called early the next morning and asked if we could meet at the office of Sir Grant. He called the office Sir Grant's chambers, but it turned out to be a suite of offices in the Middle Temple. I took James in the carry-bag, and as I entered from Fleet Street I felt an overwhelming sense of history. That very ground had been occupied for nearly a thousand years. It had been devoted to the law for the last five hundred at least. I let James out of the bag and we walked slowly along amid the old brick buildings, looking at the names posted outside the doors of the various chambers, where the solicitors, barristers and clerks who occupied each set of chambers were listed. We found Sir Grant's name. We entered and spoke to the receptionist, a young man who ushered us down a hall to a good-size room with a big desk and bookshelves on every wall. The desk was piled with papers and behind it, leaning back in his chair, was a seventy-year-old man with sparse white hair, glasses sliding down his nose, sparkling blue eyes and a mussy appearance. His tie was slightly out of line, and when he stood up to shake my hand I noticed that his coat pockets were stuffed with things. Mr. Graves was sitting primly in one corner of the room.

"Hello," said Sir Grant in a booming voice. He patted his desk. "Hop right up here, James," he went on. "I am delighted to meet you."

James sat on the end of the desk and offered a paw. Sir Grant shook it.

"Do I understand, James, that you are a witness in this case?" he asked once we were all seated.

James nodded.

Sir Grant took out a pencil whose eraser end had been chewed and prepared to make notes on a yellow pad in front of him. He kept looking at James out of the corner of his eye as Mr. Graves outlined the situation for us all.

Meanwhile, James, who had heard all this many times before, began to play with a brass figure of a bathing girl wrapped in a voluminous cloak. The brass girl was wearing a large brass hat and she was reclining on some brass sand. James patted this Edwardian beauty and she made a slight clicking sound. He patted her from the other side and the sound was repeated.

"Just a moment," Sir Grant interrupted Mr. Graves. "Look, James," he said, and flipped the cage open. It parted in two wings that revealed a brass bathing beauty without a bathing suit but still wearing her large hat. Then he flipped the wings back in place and the lady was completely covered. Sir Grant flipped the cape a time or two and then sat back to watch what James would do.

James grinned. In two tries he had the cape open. Then he shut it. He opened it again and slapped it shut and sat on the desk and purred.

"Like that?" said Sir Grant. James nodded.

"You can understand me?" asked Sir Grant seriously.

James nodded,

"You like single-malt whiskey?"

James nodded.

"You travel the world?"

James nodded.

Sir Grant was laughing now. "You like champagne and crab salad for lunch?"

James nodded vigorously.

"Wonderful," said Sir Grant. "You have a cat who knows how to nod."

James snarled. He stalked across the desk, ignoring all the papers, and to Sir Grant's surprise he slapped him on the mouth with his paw.

"Do you live in the Inner Temple?" Sir Grant asked, somewhat subdued.

James shook his head.

"Are you a marmalade cat?"

James shook his head.

"Have you been in the curator's office at the Victoria and Albert Museum?"

James shook his head.

"Have you been in the curator's office in the Huntingdown Museum?"

James nodded emphatically.

"Now I believe you," Sir Grant said after a pause.

James returned to playing with the brass lady. Sir Grant pulled his ear, chewed the end of his pencil, squinted at nothing and reset his glasses on his nose. At last he began to write. "Now our job is to get the jury to believe you, not to mention the judge. Let's get your story first."

I told Sir Grant what I had determined from James the night before. A clear picture of a man telephoning somebody named Barry, who would unload the goods. James shook his head. I tried "property" but James still shook his head. I tried "merchandise" and James nodded.

"Did he talk about money?" Sir Grant asked.

James nodded.

"A lot?"

James looked puzzled.

"A thousand pounds?" I asked.

James shook his head and waved his paw up.

"Ten thousand pounds?" I suggested. The paw waved up.

"Fifteen thousand pounds?" James nodded.

That sounded about right. There was no market in these terracotta pieces. No one knew they existed except for my small circle and Costain Cummings. They might one day be worth a million, but there was no place to fence them for anything like that at the moment. However they were sold, it would have to be to a collector who did not shout about his collection or the fraud would be uncovered. If Wentworth got £15,000, he was doing very well indeed.

So the questioning went on. Sir Grant was growing more excited by the minute.

"With this evidence there is no question of a simple mistake," he said as he put his pencil down. "Hud"—he was addressing Mr. Graves—"get someone to find out who picked up Wentworth's shipments. If we can trace one, we might get to Barry. If we can get to Barry, we will have him nailed."

Sir Grant got up and held out his hand. He took James's paw. "I can't tell you how I have enjoyed myself. You are an excellent observer and a prince of a fellow. I look forward to seeing you in court. Mr. Graves will arrange the details, but remember one thing. The defense will try to discredit you. Whatever they say, however they provoke you, do not let yourself get angry."

James nodded and bowed in a dignified way and then hopped off the desk after flipping the wings on the brassy lady one more time. We strode out together with Mr. Graves following. In the yard, surrounded by old, old buildings and rose gardens, Mr. Graves gave us our instructions for reporting to the Old Bailey and said he would be in touch.

We returned to Baron's.

"Are you worried about being a witness?" I asked as we sipped Laphroaig.

James gave me his piece-of-cake look.

The bell rang and Shep announced that he and Jane were below and would love to come up. We welcomed them. Jane was carrying a portfolio from which she extracted a number of photographs, all of James. They were prints of Tor's pictures. We stood the pictures up on the windowsill. There was James asleep on the sofa. There was James looking aristocratic. There was James arching his back, and there was James flying through the air, his paws extended, his eyes alight. It was a splendid picture. James knocked it off the windowsill. It fell on the floor and James fell on it and licked it.

"I'll tell Tor you liked it,' said Shep.

"Well," said Jane, "my client is thrilled with these pictures and so am I. I'll just run upstairs and get Mrs. March's signature on a release and pay for James's services, and this job will be complete." Jane was out the door and up the stairs, her black patent leather heels flashing as she ran.

James and Shep played roughhouse for a while and then James went back to admiring himself. When Jane came back he looked at her wistfully, waved a paw at the pictures and then pointed to himself.

"You want a set?" Jane asked, pleased.

James nodded.

"You may have these," she said, and James and I set the pictures back up on the windowsill temporarily.

"I'll get frames tomorrow," I said.

We all went off for a vegetarian dinner at the restaurant Poppy and Roger had recommended. James was not pleased, but when the proprietor let him stay, he settled for melted cheese on toast and a saucer of Soave. After all, wine comes from fruit.

We watched the evening news together. Or rather, I watched the news as James looked at his pictures and listened to the news.

There was a knock at the door. I straightened a picture on the way to answer.

"I wonder what is going to be done with them?"

James seemed totally uninterested. He took a last look at himself and headed out the door to Mrs. March.

"He's not bothering you?" she asked. "You know I got quite a lot of money for those pictures," she added confidentially.

James was practicing being dignified and unruffled and walked up to bed with his head up, placing his feet carefully from one stair to the next.

James and I were lolling about one late afternoon when the bell rang and Jane and Shep appeared. As I went to admit them I picked up an envelope that had been shoved under the door.

Jane had on a tailored white linen dress and white patent leather pumps. Shep was in his usual blue jeans and black

T-shirt with the odd message WAKE YOUR CAT UP TO PURR-PORRIDGE on the front. They were bubbling with excitement.

"We've come to watch television with you," they said. "We have five minutes before the program starts."

There was a flurry of activity as the furniture was rearranged and refreshment served, and then we were ready to watch ITV, one of Britain's commercial stations.

We were right on time. The music from *Cats International* was played and the title "Cats of London" appeared. Our documentary was about to begin. It was sponsored by the Combined Humane Societies of England.

As we expected, the program started with the dancers from *Cats International*. There was James teaching Ursula to stretch and Anne to curl, and there was Poppy making Ursula into a cat. James was riveted to the screen. When the segment faded out we all applauded, including James.

This section was followed by a short speech by one of the representatives of the Society for the Prevention of Cruelty to Animals, during which James played with the envelope I had put on the table.

The speaker disappeared and we were transported to Green Park. James stopped playing and settled down to watch. However, since he appeared only fleetingly he was not really engrossed.

The Green Park segment was interrupted by another speaker, this time a pretty girl who discussed the plight of stray and feral cats. She was followed by the footage we had taken in the market. The cat played with the mouse and the mother cat defended her kittens. All of us except James applauded. He watched, however.

A representative of the Animal Welfare League harangued us

while Shep, who was thirsty, got another Guinness, and Jane and I replenished the lemonade. James was drinking milk.

The Animal Welfare man was followed by the sequence at the warehouse. The cats fighting for the flounder in the glare of our lights was wonderfully effective. James sat in my lap shivering.

The program closed with a Royal, shown with what we were supposed to assume was a royal cat, who spoke in favor of the World Wildlife Fund and animals everywhere.

We all applauded as the credits were run. They included Shep and Tor and Moises and, to my great surprise, a consultant listed as "James of St. James's." I pointed this out to James, who gravely thanked Jane.

I moved to turn off the set.

"No, wait," said Jane.

A cheerful face appeared. "Wake your cat up each morning with delicious Purr-Porridge," said a cheerful voice. There was a brief glimpse of a table overflowing with good things to eat—fruit, vegetables, a goose, a veritable seventeenth-century still life—while the voiceover talked about vitamins and minerals and protein and roughage. Then a grey substance was presented in a cut-glass bowl with BELOVED CAT incised on the side, and a cat ate it with apparent enthusiasm.

Then the smiling face appeared again and held up a can with a dark blue label. On the label, his eyes glowing, his paws stretched in delight, was James exactly as he appeared in Tor's splendid photograph, which James himself had been licking only recently and which now hung, properly framed, in the office on the fifth floor. Across the top of the label were the words PURR-PORRIDGE in white.

"Just introduced," said the announcer. "Be the first to treat your cat to this delicious new product. You'll find it at your local pet store or supermarket."

James was off my lap and streaking for the set. He hurled himself against the front of it and managed to turn it off. He was in a flaming rage. He yowled, hissed and tried to claw Shep, whose fault he thought it was.

"What's the matter?" asked Jane. She was confused.

"James is furious at appearing in a commercial for cat food," I said as I picked up the envelope from the floor where it had fallen.

James stopped pacing long enough to nod grimly.

"That's stupid!" she said. "He looks splendid, and Mrs. March has made a nice fee out of it."

James hissed.

"Come on," said Shep, "we have things to do. Sorry you didn't like the commercial, old boy."

James snarled.

"You're just mad because you didn't get anything for yourself," said Jane as she left.

Exhausted, James lay on the table and sulked.

I opened the envelope. "This should interest you," I said.

James looked up. His eyes were dull.

"We are invited to a benefit performance of *Hunt the White Hunter*, to be followed by a gala ball."

James looked puzzled. At least I had his attention.

"A benefit is a performance where the audience pays a great deal more than the normal ticket price. The money all goes to whatever charity is sponsoring the benefit. At least, that is how it is supposed to work. In this case, the benefit is to aid some African famine victims. The tickets cost £100 each. Want to go?"

James still looked puzzled.

"You want to know about famine?" I asked.

James nodded.

"In parts of Africa, due in part to war and in part to drought, there are areas where the population has nothing to eat. The money this benefit raises, along with other funds, will be used to buy food on the world market and ship it to the starving people."

James nodded.

"Want to go?" I asked. "Lord Henry is on the organizing committee. His name is on the invitation. It's next week. This invitation was held up for some reason."

James managed a weak smile and nodded.

"Want to go out for dinner?" I asked.

James shook his head. He glared at the dark TV and stalked to the door. I let him out and watched as he sulked his way upstairs. He was deeply hurt.

James continued to fume. He refused to watch ITV at all for fear that the Purr-Porridge ad would appear, as it did frequently. If I inadvertently mentioned Jane's name, he snarled. One day he rejected two perfectly suitable tenants because one of them was carrying a magazine with a Purr-Porridge advertisement on the back page. I was secretly glad he had given up psychiatry for the moment. He would have had no patients at all.

Tickets arrived for the benefit along with a note from Lord Henry telling us he had arranged seats for all of us together at the performance and at the gala afterward. He and Helena, Poppy and Roger, James and me. There would be a seat for James and he would be admitted without trouble. The carry-bag would not be needed.

Mr. Graves called to say the case was moving along and we should be ready to appear at the Old Bailey in about two weeks. I passed all this information on to James. He only nodded.

The day before the benefit four cardboard cases of the sort canned goods are packed in were delivered to my flat. I stacked them up in the hall. Accompanying the cases was a note that read "With grateful thanks to the star of the label." It was signed Watt Wilder, vice-president of marketing, Purr-Porridge division of Universal Foods Ltd.

I would have hidden the cases and card from James. However, he was in the apartment when they arrived. He sat on top of the pile and pretended to throw up.

"I'll just throw them out," I said.

He shook his head, used the stack as a scratching post and gave me a grin.

Then Helena called. James cheered up immediately and purred for her over the phone.

"I called to tell you this benefit is very dressy," she said. "There will be lots of flash. Wear your earrings, Sir James, dear."

James smiled a real smile and as soon as Helena had rung off he ran to my closet. I followed and opened the small safe. Out came the topaz earrings. James tried them on and scampered around the sitting room, tossing his head and at last stood on the back of the easy chair and admired himself in the mirror. The earrings stayed on nicely but they were heavy.

The gala night arrived. Dressed in our best, we took a cab to the National Theater, presented our tickets and were seated. Lord Henry and Helena were already there. Lord Henry looked particularly handsome in his tailcoat and white vest, and Helena had a pearl tiara in her golden hair. She wore a blue-green chiffon float and the Haverstock pink pearl necklace and earrings. She looked radiant. Poppy and Roger came in shortly and, to my surprise, because Poppy usually doesn't pay any attention to clothes, she wore a beautifully cut topaz satin dress. She had piled her auburn hair on top of her head. She wore no jewelry but was stunning without it. Roger wore his dress clothes with assurance. James tossed his head from side to side and flashed his topaz earrings.

The Lyttelton Theater was full. The house lights dimmed. A single spot hit the center of the stage and Harry Kinyata appeared. He was dressed in a tawny leotard and carried a lion mask under his arm. He was greeted with enthusiastic applause.

He made a very impressive figure, and when he spoke his voice filled the theater with a wonderfully varied and controlled sound. He spoke of the needs of both men and animals in Africa and thanked us all for our generosity. There was an authenticity about his short speech that moved the audience. He did not give them a chance to applaud, however.

"Let's 'Hunt the White Hunter,'" he said in conclusion. The lights went out, leaving the theater in total darkness. James hopped onto my lap. I patted him.

A light appeared at the corner of the stage as the orchestra began to play. There was Ellen dressed in a crinoline, seated at a desk, writing. She said aloud, "Richard, dearest, do take care. . . ." The light faded and the stage was dark.

When the lights went up we saw Richard Burton searching for the source of the Nile.

The first half of *Hunt the White Hunter* was made up of a series of episodes, each with a different African explorer or hunter, which included some history and lots of native dances and music. Animals as well as people were portrayed. The company was beautifully trained, and Harry Kinyata, in a variety of roles—sometimes a tribal chief, sometimes a farmer, once a jackal and on a number of occasions a lion—was superb. Each section opened with Ellen, at the side of the stage, writing to various individuals. I remember her particularly as Mrs. Theodore Roosevelt writing "No more rhinos please" and as Mrs. Ernest Hemingway, not writing but saying "Not now, Ernest." The role was perfect for Ellen. She didn't have to do anything, she could read her lines and she had many costume changes. She looked splendid.

During the interval James and I stayed in our seats while the rest went out for refreshment. James was still puzzled. I began to realize that, of course, he had never seen anyone without enough food. It was rather the other way—he had seen us all, including himself after a huge delicious meal at Colombino's.

"Remember the cats who fought over the flounder," I said at last. "They were hungry cats. They don't get enough to eat. Imagine people like that."

James nodded in an offhand way. He was thinking of something. He was also shaking his head and pushing at his ears with his paws.

The second half began, and we were all absorbed in modern Africa, where modern African dance and music were featured. The performance built to a finale. We now saw for the first time the mound of grass we had seen on our tour of the theater some time ago. James was completely caught up in the musical, and when Harry Kinyata came roaring out of the grass to call the rest of Africa's animals, wearing his lion mask and giving a huge lion roar, James let out an answering howl that echoed through the theater. The lion on stage raised a paw in salute to the cat in the audience. Dancers dressed as animals gyrated on the stage, and at last the curtain fell to thunderous applause.

Harry, his mask in his hand, appeared in a spotlight again.

"Thank you for your generous reception," he said amid huge applause. He held up his hand.

"Please," he said when the audience was quiet, "we will have no curtain calls. We ask you to proceed to the restaurant for dinner. All the cast will be there in costume so you can recognize us individually and tell us in person how much you enjoyed our performance. Thank you all again." He disappeared.

The audience rose and began to leave the theater. The six of us decided to wait till the crowd was thinner.

James kept shaking his head as though something were bothering him. At last we got up to leave and found our way to the restaurant, where Lord Henry led us to our table. James found Poppy and patted her gently.

"What can I do for you, James?" she asked.

He brushed his ears. Poppy looked at him shrewdly. "These earrings are too heavy for you, aren't they?" she said.

James nodded and pointed at her.

She smiled. "Very well," she said. She took them off James's ears. He looked relieved. He pointed at her.

"You want me to have them?" she asked.

James grinned. So did Roger. Poppy put them on. They looked marvelous.

"Will you keep them?" asked Roger. There was some pleading in his voice.

"How can I refuse a gift from a cat?" said Poppy, and she grinned at Roger and tossed her head.

We drank champagne and ate adequate banquet food. There was music. There was dancing. People circulated, as did the cast of *Hunt the White Hunter*. Harry Kinyata came over to our table with Ellen on his arm. He had changed into his native ceremonial robe as tribal chief, and Ellen was dressed in a gold lamé gown with a crown of gold and lion fur on her head. She wore a large green emerald on a leather thong around her neck. She smiled remotely at us all as though she moved in a different, more rarefied world, as indeed she did. James snarled at her.

Harry Kinyata and Lord Henry are old friends because they were at Oxford together. They talked for a few minutes. Ellen remained aloof.

"You will be happy to know that Ellen has consented to become my wife," he said to us all as he was leaving to speak to the next table. We smiled our congratulations and Ellen bowed to her subjects.

When they had gone Lord Henry began to laugh. "Harry is closing *Hunt the White Hunter* after tonight's performance," he said. "The performers are all going back to their respective countries, and Harry is also returning to take up his much more important role as chief of his tribe. He is going to try to find a way to bridge the twentieth century and the old tribal culture. Ellen will be in for a great surprise. She will have all the gold and precious stones she ever wanted, and she will be one of at least four wives, and just the newest one."

James sipped some more champagne and chuckled a really evil chuckle.

At last I realized James was tiring fast, so we said good night and caught a cab home. On the way we passed a lighted billboard from which the face of a grey cat with paws outstretched invited one and all to buy Purr-Porridge. James covered his eyes.

"Did you enjoy the benefit?" I asked when we got home.

James grinned.

"Want to come in?"

James shook his head and trotted upstairs. At the turn he stopped, looked back at me and winked. He had something on his mind that pleased him. I heard him scratching on the door upstairs as I closed the door to my flat.

The next morning James scratched at my door very early. I was scarcely awake, but he was a determined cat. He stood in front of the framed photograph of himself and pointed.

"You want to see Tor?" I asked.

He shook his head. "Shep?" He nodded. He continued to point. "Jane, too?" He nodded.

"Let's see if I have this right," I said. "You want to see Shep and Jane as soon as possible."

James nodded.

"Very well," I said, "I'll arrange it." I had some misgivings. James was, at the moment, very angry with Shep and Jane, particularly Jane.

It happened that they were free and that very afternoon both of them arrived in the van, came upstairs, stumbled over the cases of Purr-Porridge and settled down for a pleasant afternoon.

However, James, steely determination in every move, hopped

onto the windowsill and pointed to the van. Then he stood in front of Shep, then Jane, then me and pointed. His last instruction concerned the cases in the hall.

"You mean you want us to put the cases in the van?" I asked. James nodded.

That was what he had in mind. Shep shrugged, gave James a grin, picked up a case and started for the elevator. We loaded the cases on the elevator. Jane and James rode down. We unloaded with difficulty and eventually got the three cases in the back of the van. James jumped in last. He was carrying in his mouth the map we had used when we photographed the cats of London. Various locations were marked on it, and I had kept it on the table as a souvenir.

James placed himself next to Shep, who was driving, and pointed to the market area where we had found the mother and kittens.

A dim light began to glow in my mind.

"James," I asked, "do you want to feed starving cats?"

James patted me gently and gave me his so-you-finally-got-it look.

Shep started the van and we moved off in the direction of the street market.

"How are we going to feed starving cats?" asked Jane.

James looked disgusted. He pointed to the cases in the back of the van.

Shep let out a howl of laughter. "Wonderful!" he exclaimed. "We're going to feed Purr-Porridge to starving cats."

James nodded.

"I still don't see," said Jane.

Shep was laughing as he drove. "You'll find out" was all he would say.

We arrived at the market site. For some reason the market was not too busy, and the nearby alleys and yards were nearly deserted. Shep parked the van and opened the top case. Each can of Purr-Porridge had a self-opening top.

James indicated that the tops were to be pulled off and left in the van. Shep set to work. James got out of the van and stood on the pavement. Shep put an open can on the street. James picked it up and carried it to a sheltered corner and laid it down. He brushed out his mouth and repeated the process, putting the open can in another protected place. James turned to Jane, who was watching, and waved at her.

"James wants you to get to work," laughed Shep.

"This is silly," said Jane. She went to work distributing cans, however.

Once Shep had started the project he was an enthusiastic leader. He called us to a halt and looked at the map.

"James," he said, "look here, there are all sorts of really devastated areas of London. Let's take our supplies there. These cats get enough out of the market."

James grinned and agreed. We packed up and set forth. Shep picked spots. James explored when we arrived and then showed us where to put the cans. After the first two or three cans, James refused to place them. He had to carry them in his mouth and he could not stand the taste.

In a deserted area James had found some skinny cats and we left some Purr-Porridge. James restrained Shep as we began to leave. He wanted to see what would happen. We sat quietly for a few minutes and watched as one or two cats sniffed the proffered cans. The first reaction was indifference. However, hunger is a powerful force and at last the cats began to eat. James nodded, satisfied, and we continued on our mission of mercy until all the cases were empty and dusk was beginning to make it hard to see.

"I'll say this for you, James," said Jane as we finished. "You may be a snob but you are certainly generous."

James gave her a small smile, the first since the commercial, stretched himself and rubbed his cheek against Shep's face.

"We're friends again?" Shep asked.

James grinned.

"I'll take care of the empty cases," said Shep as he and Jane dropped us off at Baron's. "Thanks for a great adventure."

We waved the van off and then went in. It was late.

"Come in for a little supper?" I asked.

We were in the middle of Hunter's soup and milk when Mrs. March knocked.

"My, you're late tonight, where have you been?" she asked.

"James put on a benefit," I answered.

"Oh, come now!" said Mrs. March. "You do have a sense of humor."

As he left, James shook his head and shrugged as if to say "She'll never understand."

The next day James and I went marketing. He was his old, happy self. He managed to overturn a display of Purr-Porridge with a poster showing his picture, which had been set up in Sainsbury's, but otherwise he was quite cheerful, even playful. He saw some smoked pheasant that appealed to him. Of course, I bought some.

Helena and Poppy came by in the afternoon. Helena's baby was due soon, and she and Lord Henry came to London often to see her doctor and take natural childbirth instruction. She stretched out on the sofa and Poppy sprawled in the big chair. James stretched out next to Helena, lying along her protruding tummy. Suddenly he started, turned and looked at the round mound next to him. He could see nothing. He lay down again. In no time he was up again.

Helena was laughing. "That's the baby, James dear," she said. "It's kicking inside me, and in about a month it will be ready to come out and live in the world." She took James's paws and held them against her for a minute and then released them. James, with considerable dignity, removed himself to a position near Helena's head on the arm of the sofa and continued to watch her with some suspicion.

"I have a great idea," said Poppy. "I want to marry Roger and he wants to marry me but I can't bear all his money, so I have decided that he should take as income the same amount I make, and we'll live on that and give the rest to starving Africa." She smiled at the success of her effort to solve the problem.

"Possible," said Helena, "but suppose you get pregnant and have to stop working, or you get sick, or you want to go back to do graduate work. If you have done this right, you have given all Roger's assets to a foundation and you have only one income. Suddenly your standard of living is cut in half and you prevent Roger from doing what he does brilliantly. You would feel fulfilled and he would feel useless."

"I never thought of that," Poppy admitted. "I guess we aren't suited at all, even though we have a wonderful time together. After the benefit he came back to my apartment and he's been there ever since, most of the time anyway. By the way, James," she added, patting him on the head, "thank you for the earrings. I really love them."

James was looking at Poppy Balsom through half-shut eyes. He shook his head back and forth. He clearly thinks she is eccentric. Anyone knows that wealth, preferably inherited, is a most desirable commodity without which one is forced to eat Purr-Porridge.

"Come on, Poppy," said Helena, getting up. "It's time for the three of us to go." She patted her tummy knowingly. "When does the trial start? I want to be there to see James testify," she said at the door.

"In two days," I told her, and we watched them as the elevator slowly descended.

After they left, James and I went over to Thwaites to see what was on show in the great room. There we picked up our friends and all went off to dinner at a restaurant where James is known. The conversation turned to the depredations of Mr. Wentworth. We invited Bob Scott, one of the most knowledgeable dealers in fine art in the city, and he explained the operation to us.

"I think it all started when the board of the Huntingdown decided that the museum store should not only stock reproductions of the best-known items but also sell some little-known items that lent themselves to reproduction, along with small pamphlets of information about the objects. As long as the store was selling reproductions of very famous pieces, it had a kind of protection. Scholars knew these pieces very well. They often came to see them and would recognize a fake almost immediately. But the small eleventh-century stone figure that turns out now to have been replaced with a reproduction was not at all well known and seldom looked at by anybody. I talked to Costain about it and he thinks it was the first of Wentworth's thefts."

"Doesn't the museum have some controls?" asked someone.

"Sure," said Scott. "It worked this way: The decision was made to reproduce the piece. An order was sent to pick it up from its position on display—you see those little cards in museums all the time saying "Removed for study" or such like. Then Wentworth, who is very good at what he does, by the way, made his copies and returned not the original but one of the copies to an assistant in the curator's office, who replaced it and marked the return on the appropriate form. The remaining copies would be stored for use in the shop, and the original, after a brief time, would be delivered to the dealer, who already had sold it to some collector out of the country who was willing to ask no questions. If anyone questioned the object returned to display at the time it was returned, Wentworth would say 'Oops' and send back the original. Nothing lost. All the paperwork straight. Lots of people handle the stuff, no trace. Now, thanks to our Yank friend here, the scam is over."

"Not me," I said. "It was James who found the originals."

"Yes, but why the terra-cottas?" someone asked. "Weren't they very risky?"

"Not really," said Scott. "After all, they had just been discovered. Almost no one had even seen them. On the other hand, people have been speculating about their existence for years, and there are other collectors besides old G. L. who would gladly pay almost any price and say not one word about where they came from."

He turned to me, "Could you have been fooled?" he asked.

"The reproductions were damned good," I had to admit. "It might have worked except that he didn't know about the monogram and so didn't take care to reproduce it. That's what James found. I was suspicious, but James knew."

"Well, it will be interesting to see what happens," said Scott. "There doesn't seem to be any hard evidence to counter his claim that it was all a mistake."

James smiled and lapped a little more red wine. I winked at him and he winked back, and we all finished dinner, and James and I went home to bed.

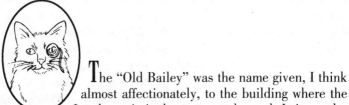

The "Old Bailey" was the name given, I think almost affectionately, to the building where the London criminal courts are housed. It is a relatively new building, square, not very attractive, not at all ornate, built on the site of the old Newgate prison. James and I presented ourselves there the next morning, with James in the carry-bag until we were in the building. We sat in the hall and waited a few minutes for Mr. Graves, who appeared neatly buttoned up with umbrella in hand, though it was a lovely summer day. He was followed shortly by Sir A. Grant Paine, Queen's Counsel (Q.C.), which means he is a very distinguished barrister. Sir Grant looked as though he had been tearing around all night. His coattails flew as he trotted along, and all his pockets were full.

He waved us a cheery good morning and disappeared.

"He must get robed," Mr. Graves explained.

"Can we go in?" I asked.

"Not till you are called. Witnesses are not allowed to listen to the testimony of others," said Mr. Graves. "Someone will come to get you at the right time."

So we sat outside the courtroom and watched the passing scene, and James took a nap until a bailiff came to get us and we entered the courtroom, where a judge in a red robe and long curly wig sat behind a large desk with a solid front on a raised platform not too different from the courtrooms in the United States. The principal difference I could see was that the spectators were not seated in the courtroom proper, but in a balcony hanging from the side of the room, so placed that the witnesses giving evidence were facing directly away from them. I had a chance to look around, and there in the visitors' balcony were Poppy and Helena and Lord Henry and about sixteen other people, all the gallery would hold.

Seated at tables in front of the judge's bench were the solicitors, Mr. Grey and his counterparts, and the barristers, who wore special white collars, gowns that looked like those worn by university graduates, and grey curly wigs with small tails hanging down. I noticed that Sir Grant's wig was always slightly askew.

James slipped into the bench where Mr. Graves was sitting, and I entered the witness box to give my testimony.

Sir Grant led me through my meeting with Costain Cummings, my bringing the statues to the museum to be photographed and my nagging to get them back. Then I described going to the office and eventually finding the statues in Mr. Wentworth's possession. I explained that the statues were now in the hands of my client in New York. Pictures of the statues were introduced. I identified them.

"You recognized immediately that the statue on Mr. Wentworth's desk was a reproduction?" asked Sir Grant.

"No," I replied, "James had already made that discovery and knocked the spurious statue onto the floor."

"Who is James?" interrupted the judge. "Can he give his own testimony?"

"I hope so, my lord," said Sir Grant, with the faintest hint of a twinkle. "He is here in the courtroom." James had quietly moved to sit on the table in front of the lawyers, where he was clearly visible.

The judge looked around the room ."Except for this witness, there is no one here who was not here when court convened this morning. Is he in the visitors' gallery? Surely not if he is to give testimony."

"Your lordship, he is sitting on the table next to Mr. Grant."

"That cat!"

"Yes, my lord."

The judge looked around. He raised his gavel to call for order but there was no noise.

"You may proceed," he said coldly.

"So James made the discovery that the statue on the desk was a reproduction and knocked it onto the floor?"

"Yes," I said. "James found the originals in a crate on the floor beside the desk. Mr. Cummings and I took them out and verified the fact ourselves. Each of Roubiliac's works, marble or terra-cotta, as far as we know, has a small, carefully hidden monogram on it. The reproductions, in addition to being a bit soft-looking, were without monogram. The originals have the monogram."

I then described the rest of our actions in taking the statues directly to Thwaites and sending them to the United States.

"Did you discuss these events with James?"

"Yes, I did at some length," I answered. "James had been sitting in Mr. Wentworth's office for some time before he summoned us. I wanted to find out what he had seen and heard."

The judge looked sternly at me. "Do I understand that you talk to this cat?" he asked.

"Yes, your honor, I mean your lordship, I talk to him frequently."

James for his part waved a paw and nodded firmly. Sir Grant gave him a sharp shake of the head. James subsided. The judge watched the exchange and so did Mr. Wentworth.

"Are the terra-cotta statues valuable?" the judge asked, still watching James.

"Yes, they certainly are," I answered.

"Did you give the museum, or Costain Cummings himself, permission to reproduce the statues?" asked Sir Grant.

"Certainly not," was my answer.

"That's all, my lord," said Sir Grant, and sat down.

"You may cross-examine," said the judge.

Another barrister in gown and wig rose from the other end of the long table.

"How many people know about these statues?" the barrister asked.

"It's hard to say. I have talked about my search to everyone I know in the art world ever since I arrived in England nearly three months ago. The more people who knew what I was looking for, the better my chances of finding it. Once I found them, I told everyone about them. My client in New York was most interested in having them photographed and documented at the Huntingdown, but not reproduced."

"Your client's collection is quite extensive, is it not?"

"Yes."

"Has he ever loaned any items to a museum or other place where the public might see them?"

"Not to my knowledge."

"So you might have sent the reproductions and kept the originals yourself without his being any the wiser, might you not?"

"I object," said Sir Grant, springing to his feet and waving an arm. "There is not the slightest shred of evidence that this was a possibility."

"I am not asking the witness whether or not he did keep the originals. I am asking him if it was a possibility."

"It was not possible for me, no," I answered.

James hissed.

The judge looked annoyed. "Do not answer the question until I have ruled on it," he said irritably.

Sir Grant glared at James.

"You may proceed Mr. Benton," said the judge.

"Who knew you were taking the statues to the Huntingdown to be photographed?" The barrister said the last word with a heavy emphasis.

"I can't say. I mentioned it to lots of people and they may have told more, certainly five or six, anyway."

"When you entered Mr. Wentworth's office you saw a statue on the desk and a partially packed crate on the floor beside the desk, is that correct?"

"Yes."

"You found the original statues in the crate?"

"Yes."

"You and Mr. Cummings asked Mr. Wentworth about the two sets of statues?"

"Yes."

"What did he tell you?"

"That he had made the copies as requested and was surprised it was the originals in the crate."

"And then you took the originals and the cat and left?"

"That's right."

"That's all." Mr. Benton sat down.

"Redirect, Sir Grant?"

"No, my lord."

"You may step down," said the judge. I returned to the lawyers' table. No one asked me to leave.

Sir Grant stood up. "My lord," he said, "I beg leave to call a most unusual witness, the cat, James, a British blue cat, property of Mrs. Hilary March."

Mr. Benton was on his feet. "I strenuously object," he said. "This is a frivolous obfuscation on the part of the prosecution. It is, in fact, one of the most outrageous affronts to the dignity of the court in the whole history of English law."

The judge smiled on Mr. Benton. "I am inclined to agree with you," he said. Then he turned to Sir Grant. "Have you any evidence to substantiate your claim that this is anything but a trained circus cat?"

"I had anticipated your lordship's concern," said Sir Grant. "I have a number of character witnesses who are willing to testify to James's abilities. Do you wish to hear them now or after the cat testifies? I believe your lordship has their names, as does opposing counsel."

The judge picked up a paper in front of him and studied it with a sigh.

"I think we'll hear the cat now," he said in a resigned voice.

Mr. Benton sat down, looking not too worried. I noticed Mr. Wentworth was looking very worried indeed, however.

"Thank you, my lord, I call James."

James, looking neither to the right nor the left, walked with great dignity to the witness box and made himself comfortable on the top of the box itself.

A bailiff produced a carton, which he put on top of the witness chair, and James sat on that, the soul of dignity.

The bailiff, greatly discomfited, presented James with a Bible and swore him in.

Sir Grant began his questioning. "Your name is James? You live at Baron's Chambers on Ryder Street?"

A nod.

"Have you ever been in a courtroom before?"

A shake of the head.

With a heavy sigh, the judge turned to the court reporter. "You will indicate 'Yes' for a nod and 'no' for a shake."

"My lord," said Sir Grant, "I suggest, in order to satisfy yourself that James is not a trained circus cat, that you ask him any questions you wish."

The judge looked taken aback but recovered.

"Do you like Purr-Porridge?" he asked.

James opened his eyes wide, hissed and shook his head vehemently.

"Well, do you know Lord Henry Haverstock?"

James smiled and nodded his head.

"I see. You may proceed, Sir Grant."

"My lord," said Sir Grant, "because of the limitations of my witness, I may have to ask him what would be considered leading questions."

"Obviously," said the judge, trying to regain control of himself.

Sir Grant then led James through finding the monogram in Westminster Abbey, seeing it on the Shakespeare terra-cotta, on the Handel marble and on the terra-cottas from Buenos Aires.

No mention was made of the fact that James had actually made the trip. Then he took James through the last visit to the museum on the day we found the reproductions.

"You heard Mr. Wentworth on the phone?"

A nod.

Mr. Benton was now quietly conferring with his client.

"Did he see you come in?"

A shake of the head.

"Did he say, 'It's a wonderful day outside'?"

A shake.

"Did he say, 'I'll meet you for dinner tonight'?"

A shake.

"Did he say, 'I'm crating them now, I'll bring them this afternoon'?"

James, looking directly at Mr. Wentworth, nodded.

"Did he say, 'I'm crating them now I'll bring them tomorrow'?"

James shook his head.

"Did he say, 'Have a check for £5,000 ready'?"

James shook his head.

"Did he say, 'Have a check for £15,000'?"

James nodded very slowly. The courtroom was very quiet.

"Did you then run back to get the curator?"

James nodded and shifted his position.

"When you got back to Mr. Wentworth's office, did you jump on his desk and after looking at the statue, quickly knock it off onto the floor?"

James nodded.

"Then did you attempt to unpack the crate?"

James nodded.

"That's all, my lord," said Sir Grant.

Mr. Benton rose to his feet. He did not look happy. "My lord," he said, "I am also going to make a singular request. I should like to cross-examine this cat in a closed room where none of the people who appear to know him are present. I propose to do this with the cat, myself and my client in an empty courtroom. I shall be delighted to have the proceedings televised and have the court in electronic communication so that Sir Grant can object to questions if he wishes and the court can watch the proceedings, but I wish the cat to be prevented from receiving any signals from anyone. I believe this whole performance is a ploy developed by Mr. Cummings to protect himself from having to answer for the aborted theft himself."

The judge sighed. "I cannot really refuse." He looked at the clock on the wall. "Bailiff, we will recess until two o'clock. Can you be ready by then?"

The bailiff nodded. We all rose and the court adjourned for lunch.

We met Lord Henry, Helena and Poppy in front of the building and all of us headed for a nearby restaurant. Sir Grant could not join us. But before he went to keep an appointment he grinned at James in a gleeful way.

"Splendid!" he exclaimed. "My only advice for this afternoon is, Don't let them make you mad whatever they do."

James smirked, waved at Sir Grant and gave us all his piece-of-cake grin.

After lunch we reassembled. I joined Lord Henry, Helena and Poppy in the visitors' gallery, which we reached by a small side entrance. The visitors' gallery is a very cramped place.

Mr. Graves was now in charge of James.

The bailiff got us all to our feet. The judge entered. We would see, placed in one corner of the courtroom, a large television set.

At the barristers' table sat Sir Grant and Mr. Graves. On the screen we could see Mr. Benton and Mr. Wentworth at their table and near them a chair. Suddenly James appeared on the screen, walking with great dignity to the chair, where he sat and waited. To one side, barely in the picture, was a court reporter and beside him a bailiff.

"Your name is James?" asked Mr. Benton.

James nodded.

"Nice kitty!" said Mr. Wentworth.

James gave him a cold stare.

"Have you ever seen this man before today?" Mr. Benton pointed to the stenographer.

James shook his head.

"Have you seen this man before today?" Mr. Benton pointed to Mr. Wentworth.

James nodded.

"When?" asked Mr. Benton sharply.

James shrugged and waited.

"Did you find any food in Mr. Wentworth's office?"

A nod.

"I had a Danish and coffee on a workbench," hissed Mr. Wentworth.

"Was Mr. Wentworth's phone yellow?"

James shook his head. He shifted his position. Mr. Wentworth held out a dish of a popular brand of kitty treats.

Sir Grant, with a twinkle in his eyes, rose to his feet. "I object," he said, "to the efforts of Mr. Wentworth to suborn my witness."

"Sustained," said the judge.

Mr. Benton gave Mr. Wentworth a black look. The kitty treats were withdrawn.

"Is Mr. Wentworth's telephone black?"

A nod.

"Was Mr. Wentworth holding the phone in his left hand?"

A nod, but James was getting restless. He stretched and lay down.

"Was Mr. Wentworth wearing a green shirt?"

James shook his head, rolled over and began batting the air. He was bored.

Sir Grant rose to his feet. "My lord," he said in a loud voice. James looked up and appeared to be less bored.

"My lord," said Sir Grant, "I think we have tested the ability of James to observe, quite enough."

"Sustained," said the judge. "Please confine yourself to substantive questions."

"You don't like Mr. Wentworth, do you?"

James shook his head.

"You have made up this story to protect Mr. Cummings, haven't you?"

James shook his head. He looked angry.

"Isn't it true that you are really a tool of Mr. Cummings?"

James shook his head.

"Isn't it true you are a thief yourself? Didn't you plan to help Mr. Cummings substitute the reproductions for the originals?" Mr. Benton was making a wild stab.

James had proved an unbreakable witness, but now James broke. After all, he had stolen the thistle brooch from Ellen. Without realizing it, Mr. Benton had hit a raw nerve.

James arched his back. Hissed and then howled. The noise racketed through the courtroom. On the tiny screen Mr. Benton tried to calm the cat. James, claws unfurled, struck out. Mr. Benton retreated. Remembering where he was, he turned to the camera and said, "I have no further questions." It was clear no one would have any more questions for the moment.

Court was temporarily recessed. Sir Grant went to the cross-examination room to collect his witness, who was sitting dejectedly on the witness chair. Mr. Benson and Mr. Wentworth had gone.

I found James and Sir Grant eventually.

I explained to Sir Grant about the brooch.

"So, you see, James has stolen something himself," I said.

"James," said Sir Grant, "you are a great cat. There is no question that the jury believes in you. Now, the only question is what they believe. Are you a conspirator of Mr. Cummings, or Mr. Wentworth's avenging angel? I'll put my money on the latter, but time will tell. Be of good cheer, old dear."

James was not to be mollified. He was sure the case was lost.

Sir Grant returned to court and the judge recessed the case until the following day when the defense would call its witnesses and closing arguments would be given.

We all went off to tea at the Savoy, but James was depressed, and even a generous helping of Devonshire cream with orange marmalade, which he greatly prefers to strawberry jam, did not lighten his gloom. He refused to join me for supper but went straight to bed.

The next morning we arrived early to get a good seat in the visitors' gallery. We had to run through a group of press photographers who were waiting to take James's picture, but we made it in good time and we were all sitting in the front row when the judge was announced and the trial continued.

Mr. Benton called Mr. Wentworth, who took the stand and testified that he had done his job of making reproductions of pieces in the museum collection for sale in the museum store.

Pieces were sent to his department with an order signed by the curator or the head of a particular department. Once the work was completed, he returned the original either to the curator or, on frequent occasion, directly to the spot from which the object had been taken in the first place.

"How did you come to have these statues?" asked Mr. Benton.

"I received a note to go to Photography to get them along with a request that I make reproductions of them. I showed my authorization to the girl at Photography and she gave me the statues and I signed a receipt."

"Now tell us about the day the—cat"—the word was said with great distaste—"came into your office and found the statues."

"Well, I was preparing to return the originals to Photography, where they came from, and I put what I thought were the copies in a crate to send to the shop. I am very sorry about the mistake. I don't usually make mistakes, but these copies are very good and I just moved too fast."

James was hissing. I calmed him as best I could.

"Were you talking on the phone before the curator came in?"

"Certainly not."

"Have there ever been any problems of this sort before?"

"Never."

"Are you on good terms with Mr. Cummings?"

"I think he is jealous of my skill."

"No further questions." Mr. Benton sat down.

"You may cross-examine," said the judge.

Sir Grant rose. "You have given an admirable picture of your procedures. Do you know any reason why Photography did not tell the curator the statues had been sent to Reproduction?"

"I didn't even know they didn't tell him. It's only his word."

"Do you usually send your reproductions to the museum shop in wooden crates?"

Mr. Wentworth thought for a moment.

"Well," he said at last, "not usually."

"Most of the time you keep a stock of reproductions in your shop and send one or two upstairs in a paper bag, or just carry them, isn't that right?"

"I suppose so," said Mr. Wentworth.

"So, why the heavy wooden crate, secure enough to transport the statues on a long airplane flight if necessary, just to carry them upstairs?"

"I wanted to be extra careful."

"With copies you could replace at any time?"

"I trust I am not to be persecuted for being overcareful," said Mr. Wentworth in a righteous voice.

"Have you ever used a wooden crate to transport copies before?"

"Not recently."

"Ever?" insisted Sir Grant.

"I guess not," said Mr. Wentworth.

"Is £15,000 a fair price for a pair of statues sold to a fence?" said Mr. Grant in an offhand voice.

"I think it's too little, myself," said Mr. Wentworth. "I have no idea where the cat got that idea."

"You were not happy about it?"

"No," said Mr. Wentworth, and suddenly gasped.

"Nothing further," said Sir Grant.

On redirect Mr. Benton led Mr. Wentworth to say that the matter of the money was entirely speculation, as no specific reference had been made to money ever. Then Mr. Wentworth was excused. No more witnesses were called, and Mr. Benton rose to make his closing argument, which rested on the fact that Mr. Wentworth had made a terrible mistake, but mistakes were not criminal. The originals had been found and were now in the hands of their rightful owner, and perhaps it was the curator who had larceny at heart. Mr. Benton finally suggested that, as a part of a vendetta against Mr. Wentworth, the curator had resorted to using a cat as a witness, a clearly frivolous gesture. The case should be thrown out of court.

Sir Grant rose to give his argument.

"Ladies and gentlemen of the jury," he said, "there is only one area of disagreement between Mr. Benton and myself. The Crown acknowledges Mr. Wentworth's skill as a technician. However, we contend that Mr. Wentworth, and only Mr. Wentworth, deliberately planned to return to the curator the reproductions he had made and then sell the originals through a confederate to whom he was talking on the telephone when James overheard him. For this purpose he was packing the statues in a large wooden crate suitable for transport over long distances.

"We are not asking you to *assume* that these were the true events. We ask you to believe our witness. If you believe James, Mr. Wentworth is guilty. James is a very unusual witness, but I submit that he is totally credible, and I think you will think so too."

James waved a paw. I grabbed it and curbed him.

"If you believe James," Sir Grant continued, "the problem of the crate used to transport two small statues one floor in a museum is solved. If you believe James, Mr. Wentworth's concern for the value of the statues is reasonable. I suggest he is not happy with the amount his confederate offered. If you believe James, the concern of the curator that the Photography Department took so long is reasonable. It is up to you. I am confident you will find the truth."

Sir Grant sat down. The judge instructed the jury, which was led away by the bailiff. Court was recessed.

Sir Grant swept us all off to lunch at his club.

"Whatever the outcome, the jury won't return until sometime late this afternoon," said Sir Grant as we sat around a table sipping good single-malt whiskey. "They plan to have lunch at the Crown's expense, believe me. I don't think they will take too long, once they get to work, whether they believe you, James, or whether they don't."

James lapped a little whiskey but looked downcast.

"Don't worry, James," said Sir Grant as we ate grilled plaice. "I'm not worried. I know you lost your temper, but in a way that's in our favor. A trained circus cat would not have responded that way." James looked somewhat mollified.

Sir Grant kept us all entertained with tales of some of his more obscure cases. We had just finished some quite acceptable trifle when a waiter came up with a message that the jury was returning shortly, and we hurried off to get seats in the visitors' gallery.

In half an hour, the barristers and solicitors and other officials of the court began to enter the courtroom, and shortly the bailiff called "All rise" as the judge entered and took his seat.

The jury was ushered into the box.

"Have you reached a verdict?" the judge asked.

"We have," said the foreman.

"The accused will rise and hear the verdict," said the judge.

"We find the defendant guilty as charged," read the foreman in a clear voice.

James let out a long sigh of relief. Sir Grant gave a quick look at us in the gallery and winked.

Mr. Wentworth looked up at James and glared.

The judge thanked the jury, gave Mr. Wentworth over to a sergeant who would deliver Mr. Wentworth, now a prisoner, to the proper authorities, and the rest of us left.

James, Lord Henry, Helena and I all got in a cab and returned to Baron's Chambers. We had barely gotten Helena settled on the sofa when Peter Hightower arrived to hear all about the trial.

We watched the early evening news together, where the trial and its outcome were reported. James was seen walking along beside Sir Grant on our way to lunch, and there were more pictures of Sir Grant and Mr. Benton and Mr. Wentworth.

James seemed pleased but there was something on his mind. I could not tell what it was, but he let a Purr-Porridge commercial get by him as I searched for another version of the news.

He shook his head when we asked him to join us for dinner and walked up the stairs in an abstracted way.

The newspapers played up the story the next day and James appeared on the front page. Oddly enough no one made the connection between the big grey Purr-Porridge cat and the "star witness" in the museum case. James made me cut his picture out and paste it on the bathroom mirror before he went off to work at Thwaites.

I went to the Huntingdown to talk to Costain Cummings, interrupting him as he was discussing a complete revision of the museum system for handling valuable items.

"When the staff is honorable any adequate referencing protocol will suffice, but when a malefactor is inserted in the organization, it is almost impossible to detect that malefactor until he commits some predation," he said with a sigh.

"I'm curious about the first piece Wentworth took," I said. "I understand it was a small eleventh-century stone carving of a madonna and child from Byzantium. Am I right?"

"Yes," said Costain, "it is—I should say, was, because we have no indication in whose hands the original now resides. It is a delicate and impressively primitive piece of work. Once we placed reproductions of it in the shop, it met with immediate acceptance and increased the interest in the few eleventh-century pieces we have. It was because of this renewed interest we discovered that the original had been filched."

"I want to buy one of the copies," I said. "In my business I see a great many private collections. I certainly didn't expect to run across the Roubiliac terra-cottas in Buenos Aires, but I did, so who can tell what I might find next, and I need to study this piece so I'll recognize it."

"You shall certainly not purchase it," said Costain.

He opened a drawer of his desk and took out an object about the size of an ordinary paperback book. It was made of a stone aggregate that gave the appearance of old weathered limestone. It was indeed a charming relief carving designed to be used as a devotional piece in a small shrine in a house. In a fairly dim light it was convincingly old-looking.

"Help yourself to it," said Costain. "And if the deity who shelters museum curators is feeling warmly toward me, perhaps he will put the original in your way."

"I hope so," I said.

A little later I said farewell to my friend and left him to his reorganization, which, as he said, would work till someone took advantage of it someday in the future.

When I got back to Baron's, I showed the stone piece to James and told him about it. He studied it carefully. Then I put it into my jacket pocket and forgot it.

The next afternoon Peter Hightower came by and brought Sir Grant with him. They happen to be old friends and are much alike, though Sir Grant is a little larger in frame and much less well turned out. It is not that Sir Grant's clothes aren't well tailored, but he is almost always in motion and gradually his shirt bunches up, his tie is loosened and his hair, what there is of it, stands on end.

We all drank Lagavulin and I opened a can of Strasbourg pâté on James's instructions.

James lay on the coffee table looking at Sir Grant, who was sitting on the sofa.

"James hasn't been himself since the trial," I said.

Sir Grant looked at him affectionately. "You are a sensitive soul, aren't you?"

James nodded.

"I thought I'd come to tell you what has happened," he said. "Once the verdict was in, for which we have you to thank, James, things moved very fast. The museum examined its collection and found that not only the eleventh-century piece but some other pieces had been forged. None of any very great importance, I'm happy to say. The Byzantine piece is the only one to feel sad about. However, small bits of evidence began to emerge and at last Wentworth threw in the sponge and confessed. There will be no appeal. However, the dealer to whom he sold his pieces has, as one might expect, left the country. In fact he did so the very day you intercepted the delivery of the terra-cottas. There is no way to get him. We are not even sure the name he used when he bought things from Wentworth was his real name. As for the collectors who have these pieces, there is no way in the world to find them."

James was looking very troubled.

"Come here," said Sir Grant.

James sat on his lap.

"Are you worried about Wentworth?"

James shook his head.

"The museum?"

James dismissed the museum.

"The collector then?"

James nodded and looked very unhappy.

"You want to get him?"

James nodded.

"So do I," said Peter Hightower, "but it is very difficult. We have a problem at Thwaites when an object comes in for auction that we suspect may have been stolen. We can insist on a provenance, or history of ownership on the item if it is very expensive, but bills of sale can be and often are forged. Lists of stolen property are good only for a short time."

"The collector who never shows, who gloats over his stuff in private and lives for some thirty years or more with his hoard, is impossible to catch," added Sir Grant.

James shook his head.

"I know it's not fair, but it is the way of the world," said Sir Grant.

"By the way," said Peter, "gossip says the Byzantine piece is still in England. Maybe one of these days it will turn up."

"However," said Sir Grant, saluting James, "you were indeed a rare weapon in the cause of justice. You have made a splendid contribution!"

James smiled and began to purr on Sir Grant's lap.

We talked a while longer and then Peter asked us to go to his club for dinner, so we popped around the corner to the East India Club, where James is welcome, for some bubble and squeak, and a bit of spotted dick and a bottle or two of excellent claret.

The next day Helena called to invite James and myself down to Haverstock Hall for the weekend. We happily accepted. Poppy was to come by to pick us up, as Roger would already be there. The following afternoon, which was sunny and warm, I tucked my most serviceable jacket, the one I had been wearing when I last saw Costain, in my weekend bag and James and I were driven in Poppy's old car to the Hall. It was a little more crowded than the station wagon, but Poppy is a slower driver than Weatherby, so James was happy. In fact he fell asleep.

We found the Hall unchanged and Helena and Lord Henry happily and lazily awaiting the new addition.

After one of Cook's delicious dinners, we sat on the grass where we had played croquet and enjoyed the long sunset and twilight of midsummer.

The conversation was desultory. James was playing with a leaf that had drifted onto the lawn.

"I've got an exciting job coming up in a week in Stockholm," said Poppy. "I have been asked to design the costumes for a great pageant to be held on the 360th anniversary of the death of Gustavus Adolphus, the noted Swedish king. It will be particularly interesting because James I of England acted as peacemaker to end two wars during G. A.'s reign. The period is roughly 1610 to 1630. Anyway, I'm looking forward to it. I have been making sketches and doing research, and during this trip I'll see some rehearsals and arrange for the construction of the designs and that sort of thing."

Roger sighed. "Oh, dear . . . ," he started to say. James, who had stopped playing when he heard his second king mentioned, jumped on Roger's lap and pressed his paw against Roger's mouth so all that came out was a mumble.

Roger looked at James, nose to nose. James shook his head. No one was paying attention except me.

For a moment Roger looked mystified, then he grinned.

"May I go with you?" he asked. "I'd like to tag along as Mr. Poppy Balsom."

"Would you?" asked Poppy, surprised and delighted. "I thought you had business you had to attend to."

"I do," said Roger—James clawed his thigh—"but I think this is far more important."

James gave him a grin and wandered off to a garden bed to look for something more interesting than a leaf to play with. The ground was dry and he found a dusty spot.

While Poppy went off to get her sketches to show us, I wandered over to where James was making patterns in the dust. Roger followed.

James had drawn what appeared to be some letters. There was the monogram PBH. There was the monogram RH. James wiped them both out with a wave of his paw. Then very carefully he drew PB and RHB. He sat on his haunches and grinned.

Roger looked at the new monograms very carefully. Then he grinned.

"James," he said, "I think you are a genius."

James looked down modestly, erased the dusty drawings and trotted off about his business.

The next day dawned cool and overcast. We were all sitting around the breakfast table when Wilson announced a visitor. It was Fiona Wettin.

"Come have coffee and some of Cook's wonderful coffee cake," said Helena. "How nice to see you."

Fiona blushed. "I can't stay," she said. "I've come to collect whatever you are willing to donate to the church jumble sale, which is coming up soon. I've agreed to take on the chairmanship; after all, it is the duty of us privileged ones to shoulder the major responsibilities."

Helena started to get up. Lord Henry restrained her. "I'll have Wilson put together a nice donation and see it is delivered to the church this weekend," he said.

"Thank you, Lord Henry," said Fiona, and started out.

"Going in the direction of the village?" I asked.

"Yes," said Fiona.

"Come on, James, let's go for a walk. I have some errands to do and I would love the company. I can even help you carry things," I added to Fiona.

James did not look thrilled but he agreed. I got my jacket and once we were out on the road he bounded around happily. He headed up a driveway a little distance down the road and disappeared. Soon he reappeared, obviously with something on his mind. We arrived at that driveway.

"I'll leave you here," said Fiona. "I'm going to see if Isabel has anything for me."

James was waving his tail in the direction of the driveway.

"Could I come along?" I asked. "I might be able to help carry things."

"Good of you," said Fiona. "I could introduce you to Isabel as the great art expert. Her brother is a collector of all kinds of art, though he never shows his collection."

James was racing ahead of us, disappearing and then running back to see if we were still coming. Round a curve in the driveway appeared a huge, ugly Victorian house. Fiona marched up the steps and rang the bell. James stood beside her, as tense as I have ever seen him.

A maid opened the door and right behind her appeared a plump, white-haired little woman.

"Fiona Wettin!" she exclaimed in a high piping voice. "Come in, come in, all of you. What an adorable cat."

James was bent on seduction for some reason. He gave Isabel his melting look and purred as she stroked him.

"You are a pretty girl," Isabel cooed as we were ushered into a sitting room filled with bric-a-brac and elaborate furniture.

I was introduced as the great American art expert come to offer help to the British Museum.

"Oh, dear," piped Isabel, "I'm so sorry Hesketh isn't here. He is in Paris for the week. He has a fabulous collection and almost no one ever sees it."

"What does he collect?" I asked.

"Medieval art, primarily—at least I think so. I'm not much interested myself."

James, who had made no objection to being called a "pretty girl," was wandering around the room. Out of the corner of my eye I could see he was particularly interested in a door at one side of the fireplace.

"Dora, bring coffee and cake," said Isabel to the maid who had responded to a ring.

"Right away, mum," said Dora.

"I'm sure our expert would love to see the collection!" said Fiona. Here was a splendid opportunity to show how influential she was, and Fiona was not about to pass up the chance.

James, over by the inconspicuous door, nodded.

"I'd love to see it," I said eagerly, though not too eagerly, "if it is no trouble?"

"Oh dear, I don't know," said Isabel. "Hesketh is very fussy about it. He might not like it if I showed it without his permission."

James, trying to look like a pretty girl, left the door and came to rub himself against Isabel's legs. She picked him up.

"You darling cat, do you think it would be all right?" James lolled in her arms, looked into her eyes and nodded wistfully. He rubbed his chin against her cheek.

"All right, I'll do it," said Isabel, still clutching James. At that moment cake and coffee arrived, so we ate and drank and James continued to be a "pretty girl," though I could see he was really tense underneath it all.

At last Isabel got up and went to the door by the fireplace and tapped a code into a panel of buttons next to the handle. Then she opened the door.

"These rooms are protected with all sorts of alarms and connections to the police," she said.

Fiona poked her head into the unlighted room. "Just old stuff," she said. "Come along, Isabel, we'll leave the expert and get some jumble."

James streaked into the room. Isabel and Fiona departed, leaving me in the first of a series of large rooms filled with an incredible accumulation of icons, stone carvings, swords, shields, jewelry, armor and more from about A.D. 4 to 1300. The objects were not organized or identified; it was a sort of miscellany of very valuable things that were hung on the walls and placed on tables throughout the rooms. Tall windows that extended from floor to ceiling were heavily barred as well as taped for electronic surveillance. I was awed, as much by the mass of the accumulation as by its quality. I looked for James. He was standing by a low table next to one of the windows. Then I saw why. On the table was a Byzantine stone-carved relief of a madonna and child about the size of a paperback book. The original, which had been stolen from the Huntingdown! I was stunned for a moment. Casually I put my hand in my jacket pocket—the same jacket I had worn when I went to see Costain. I felt something. I pulled the reproduction out of my pocket. James yowled.

"Shh," I said. Then I placed the reproduction on the table and placed the original in my pocket.

James was turning somersaults.

I heard Isabel and Fiona returning.

I moved away from the table, and when they came into the room I was standing in front of a mosaic, apparently lost in admiration.

"I know we must move on," I said, "but I cannot express my gratitude for this opportunity. You brother has amassed a quantity of wonderful things."

Isabel ushered us out of the room, closed the door and punched all the appropriate buttons.

"It was a pleasure to meet you and your adorable cat," said Isabel at the door. "I should suggest that a blue bow on her neck would look lovely." James bowed.

As we walked down the drive I looked back at the house. The windows of the rooms housing the collection were covered with trees, but from James's level he could see into them with ease. He had spotted the carving and led me to it.

Fiona had a box for herself and another for me to carry, so I followed her to the basement of the village church, said good morning to the vicar and at last was able to escape to hurry back to the Hall.

As soon as I was in the house, I made for the nearest phone. I reached Costain Cummings at his home.

"I have your stone madonna," I said without preamble.

"Impossible," said Costain. "You're inebriated."

I told him of my adventure. He began to laugh.

"I'm not surprised. That man spreads an evil odor wherever he goes in the collecting world. He will never be able to do anything about it when he finds his stone madonna is a reproduction. He will know the difference immediately when he looks at it. He may be an unprincipled collector, but he is superbly educated." Costain was jubilant.

"James found it," I said, "but more important, how do I get it back to you? I don't want it in my jacket pocket any longer than is necessary. That's where it is now."

"I am sending the assistant curator for it immediately," said Costain. "It will take him about an hour to get to the Hall, then he will come right back to the museum, and it will be installed this very afternoon. I am forever your humble, obedient servant."

True to his word, in an hour a car drove up, and the stone madonna was delivered to Costain's assistant, whom I knew by sight. Later that afternoon I had a call confirming that the lady with her child was back where she belonged.

At dinner I told the whole story.

"A combination of luck and purposefulness," said Lord Henry, who was feeling philosophical. "You put the reproduction in your jacket pocket and forget it there. You do remember to bring the jacket on a beautiful summer day because the weather report predicts cold, and for once the report is correct, and you put on your jacket when you go for a walk. It just so happens that the house where the original has landed is almost next door. James sees the stone piece and leads you to the exchange. Some of it is just dumb luck."

"We'll never finish this discussion," said Helena, yawning. "I'm for bed."

When our lady commands we obey, so we all went to bed.

James and I looked out the window of our room. A wind was blowing and clouds were scudding across the stars. It was growing faintly warmer.

James was purring.

"We ought to be ashamed of ourselves," I said in what tried to be a very stern voice. "Do you realize we broke all the rules? We seduced poor Isabel, we violated her hospitality after eating her cake and drinking her coffee, and then we stole a valuable antique."

James yowled with glee. He leapt with a flying leap all the way to the bed, where he rolled over and over making little happy noises and patting his paws together.

"Okay," I said, laughing with him. "Not another word, ever, about breaking the rules," and we fell happily asleep.

The next morning at early breakfast before we were to leave for London, Roger dropped a not unexpected bombshell.

"Poppy has agreed to marry me," he said.

"Yes," Poppy interrupted. "You see, Roger has agreed to become Roger Ham Balsom and I'll stay Poppy Balsom. That way we're even. He has all the money, I have the name."

James winked at Roger. Roger winked back, and pictures of monograms in the dust floated through my mind.

"However," Poppy went on, "I am determined to give the wedding. It's the responsibility of the bride's parents, and since neither Roger nor I have living parents, I'll do it myself."

"We plan to go to a registry office and do the legal stuff," said Roger, taking up the tale, but not for long.

"Then we'll have a ceremony of our own," Poppy broke in, "because neither of us belongs to a church, and we'll have a picnic with you all, and Shep and Ursula and Anne and Jane and a few of Roger's friends, and then we'll be off to Stockholm for work and a wedding trip at the same time."

Helena clapped her hands in delight and the rest of us cheered. James was sniffing around everyone's plate to see if there was any leftover Hollandaise sauce from the eggs Benedict we had been served for breakfast. He wore his I-knew-it-all-the-time look.

"May I offer Haverstock Hall as the venue?" asked Helena. "I will let you provide everything and do it any way you want, but I should not have to go out, and if it is a beautiful day, we'll use the garden and if not, we can be inside."

Poppy and Roger consulted. "Wonderful!" they exclaimed in unison.

"Next Saturday we'll be married," Poppy said firmly, and then looked at Roger. "Is that all right?" she asked.

He hugged her. "Next Saturday, and we'll return to London that night and leave for Stockholm early Sunday morning."

There was much discussion of a general sort and then Weatherby appeared, and James and I were stowed in the wagon and Poppy and Roger were stowed in her little car, and off we went to London for the week.

That very afternoon Poppy and Roger stopped in. "We need some advice," said Roger, once they were comfortable.

"We don't want a minister at our wedding," said Poppy.

"We are writing our own ceremony," said Roger.

"But we do need some sort of leader," said Poppy.

"To sort of start and stop things," said Roger.

"But we don't want to single out any one friend above the others," said Poppy. "It wouldn't be democratic."

"But we want someone important to us, not just anyone."

James, who had been listening to all this, meowed. Poppy and Roger looked at him. He pointed to himself.

The principals looked at each other.

"What do you think, Mr. Balsom?" asked Poppy, and they both burst out laughing and fell into each other's arms.

When they recovered, they agreed that James was the perfect person to be the master of ceremonies at the wedding.

Eventually we went off to the vegetarian restaurant that was Poppy and Roger's particular enthusiasm at the moment and had dinner. James was so full of himself and his accomplishments and the prospect of becoming a practicing minister, he ate half my nut loaf before he remembered he hated nut loaf. I contributed a bottle of the best champagne, and James, who loves champagne, was blissful.

The week flew by. Poppy and Roger stopped in to rehearse a couple of times, Peter Hightower came to visit and took us off to his club for dinner. It was a special occasion. Peter was leaving almost immediately for Malta and I was due to leave shortly after the wedding for the United States.

"Want to go to Malta, James?" Peter asked at dinner. James shook his head. He does not really like riding under a blanket for long periods of time.

As we left I thanked Peter for all his help and wished him well on his travels.

Shep and Jane came by. Shep and James played noisily as usual. James has a new game. Shep sits in a straight chair with his back to the windows. James climbs on the sill and launches himself at Shep's back in an attempt to push him over. It is a vigorous game. Occasionally chairs are overturned.

Jane, neat as usual in bright green linen, watched for a while.

"Calm down, you two," she said at last.

James looked at her suspiciously.

"I have news, James," she said. "First, you will not have to see yourself as the Purr-Porridge salesman any longer. It seems all cats hated it as much as you did, so it is off the market."

James grinned at Jane.

"Item two," she went on. "Remember the picture of you lying on the glass table, all stretched out with your eyes half closed and just faintly smiling?"

James nodded.

"Well," she said triumphantly, "what do you think of this?" She held up the artwork for an advertisement for a diamond bracelet, which was cleverly superimposed on the recumbent cat.

James looked at it for a long time. He patted it. He paced the table. At last he nodded his head.

"It's okay?" Jane asked.

James nodded.

Shep roared. "You snob, James. You hate to see your picture associated with cat food, but diamond bracelets are fine!"

James shrugged and sat on the table looking dignified.

Jane ran up to the fifth floor on her green patent-leather pumps and got Mrs. March's signature on another contract, and then we all went out to dinner.

Early Saturday morning, Shep and Jane arrived in the van, which was full of baskets and boxes, to take us and our suitcase (as we were spending the night) off to Haverstock Hall for the wedding. The day was warm and sunny, not a cloud anywhere.

When we got to the Hall we found Poppy and Roger were already in the yard where we had played croquet. Behind the croquet court, now a simple lawn, was a flower bed with masses of roses and behind them, a group of holly trees. The Haverstock gardeners had arranged a sort of chicken-wire arch about seven feet high in front of the holly trees and roses. Poppy and Ursula, her maid of honor, were filling this arbor with greens and flowers. In the center of the arbor was a six-foot stepladder.

James ran across the lawn, climbed the ladder and sat on the top step looking out over everyone. He stood up. He fit perfectly. He nodded, pleased with the arrangement and then ran down the ladder again. A gardener appeared with a metal frame designed to hold flower pots. It was full of pots of ivy and philodendron that trailed down the frame and completely hid the stepladder.

Roger and Shep began to set up folding chairs on the grass in a pattern that formed an aisle leading from the French windows in the library.

At one side of the lawn, Lord Henry, Anne, Jane and two of Roger's friends were setting up the buffet on a series of card tables provided by Wilson and covered in green cloths.

The day was very warm.

The bower and tables were finished. The chairs were all arranged. The principals retired to change.

At one-thirty, Anne appeared with her guitar. She has a lovely voice, and as a prelude she played a variety of classical guitar pieces with skill and feeling. We all assembled. When we were all seated, she began to sing Handel's "Where'er You Walk." At that signal we all stood up.

James came out from the library up the aisle, walking with great dignity, his tail in the air, his head erect. He was followed by Ursula in an apricot organdy dress. She carried a bunch of yellow daisies. From behind the holly trees, Roger and his best man, Fred, appeared.

Poppy followed Ursula in a simple dress of white organdy over a very pale blue slip. Her wonderful auburn hair was piled high on her head and covered with an antique lace mantilla, which Helena had found in one of the Haverstock trunks. She was perfectly happy and perfectly beautiful.

James had disappeared behind the arbor for a fleeting moment only to appear in his niche.

The music stopped. The four participants faced the bower.

James, atop his concealed ladder, bowed to us all. We sat down. James turned to Ursula. She, in turn, faced us.

"Dear friends," she said, "Poppy and Roger welcome you to their wedding. They have written the ceremony themselves." Then she stepped to one side.

James turned to Fred and nodded.

Fred explained that Roger had decided to take Poppy's name and that after the wedding he would be known as Roger Ham Balsom. This move had already been legalized and was registered at Somerset House. He added that the presence of James as the official at the services was a tribute to his skill as a matchmaker. Then Fred stepped aside.

James beamed down on Poppy and Roger and nodded.

The participants had written a very moving service for themselves in which they promised to love and respect each other and care for each other for as long as they lived. There was no mention of obedience. They exchanged rings. They kissed. Then they faced us, stood shoulder to shoulder and Poppy said, "I now greet you as Mrs. Poppy Ham Balsom." Roger looked surprised and pleased. He had not expected this.

"I greet you as Roger Ham Balsom," he said.

Anne played a lively dance on her guitar, and James stood on his hind legs and waved his paws in celebration and began to fall off the top of the ladder. Roger caught him and the three of them danced down the aisle back to the library.

They reappeared instantly and we all rushed off to congratulate the happy couple. Shep carried James around on his shoulder to find food. The guests then attacked the buffet tables where

Poppy had provided a delicious spread. We drank chilled Chablis and tart lemonade and the day grew sultry. Poppy, in lieu of extra tables, had provided sheets, which were spread on the lawn, and the guests ate sitting on the sheets or sitting in chairs. Helena was permitted a lounge chair. The Haverstock heir was almost ready to arrive and she was somewhat unwieldy.

James left Shep and came to join Anne and me. We were sitting on a sheet. Anne had her guitar beside her. James rubbed his cheek against Anne's.

"I had no idea you were so good at the guitar and had such a splendid voice," I was saying when James arrived.

Anne laughed. "I've been a folk singer and guitarist for years," she said. "I've also been working at being a dancer, but I'm short and stocky, so I never got anywhere. But I wanted to be a dancer. *Cats* was my last effort. Then James here"—she stroked him affectionately—"showed me how to turn this short, stocky body into an asset, and so I got a dancing part, my first and, I think, my last."

"No more dancing?" I asked.

"No," she said. "James helped me become content with myself. I'm going back to singing and playing, where tall, thin, short, fat doesn't matter."

We heard Shep shout and got up to go watch Roger and Poppy cut the wedding cake. We toasted the bride and groom in champagne. The happy couple went inside to change and came out, got into Poppy's car and drove off amid a shower of rice.

Not too long after that, the rest of the guests left. Wilson and his staff removed the remains of the wedding feast, and Helena, Lord Henry, James and I lay on the lawn in the soggy heat.

"It certainly is a weather breeder," said Wilson as he carried the last of the chairs into the house.

Helena was panting. It was very still, hot and humid.

"Only a week to go," said Helena, patting her middle. "It's really eager to see the world."

A long way away there was a faint roll of thunder.

By nine o'clock we were all in bed after a simple supper of leftovers.

James and I lay in bed in the dusky light that is the late evening in England in the summer. Some clouds had appeared but it was still very hot and we were too elated to sleep.

"Just imagine," I said. "Hesketh gets home, looks at his beloved collection and sees that the eleventh-century stone madonna is a reproduction. He'll be wild."

James lay on his back and waved his paws.

"There will be nothing he can do, either," I gloated. "He can never admit he has the piece. The museum has announced the return of its stolen property and Wentworth is in jail."

There was a faint flash of lightning. A small swirl of wind moved the curtains at the open window. Then it was still again.

"What a heartwarming wedding," I mused. "I think that bride and groom will live happy ever after, unlike Ellen and Harry Kinyata. He'll live happily but she won't. See what happens when you break the rules?" I sounded off.

James sat on my chest and gave me a fierce glare.

"All right," I laughed and rolled him off my chest as I got up to look out the window. There was something in the air. I couldn't settle down to sleep—the mutterings of faraway thunder and occasional gusts of wind were disturbing. I picked up a book and started to read. James lay on the bed with his head under the sheet.

It was suddenly dark outside and the lightning was brighter. The wind was picking up. It swirled around, twisting the tops of the trees. Thunder rolled frequently. James was uneasy. He stayed on the bed and tried to burrow under a pillow.

It had started to rain. I closed the window. The wind increased. This was no ordinary summer storm. Lightning crackled intermittently and the thunder followed almost immediately. The wind was howling by now. James was cowering and I was feeling very uneasy myself.

There was a great flash of lightning and a crash of thunder, and the bedside light went out. There followed the sound of a tree falling in the howling wind and rain.

There was a momentary lull. I heard a knock at the door. It was Johnson, one of the footmen, with a flashlight. With the light from the torch I found some matches and lighted the candles on the mantelpiece.

"I think there is another flashlight in the cupboard here," said Johnson.

We looked and found a big lantern whose batteries were in good shape. It gave a powerful light.

"I must see that things are safe in the rest of the house," he said.

"James," I called, "I'm going to help Johnson."

I need not have bothered. James was right beside me.

We went out into the hall.

We found Lord Henry at the end of the hall carrying a candle.

Thunder crashed. In the next lull Lord Henry said, "I'm very worried about Helena. I think she is going to deliver."

Wilson appeared in the hall, fully dressed and carrying a flashlight.

"I think Lady Haverstock is going to have her baby," said Lord Henry. "Thank God for all the hours we spent training for this. Let's prepare the kitchen. It has a big, serviceable table and can be kept clean. There is no way we are going anywhere in this storm."

"You are right about that," said Wilson firmly. "Weatherby just came in to report that a tree is down right across the main garage door, and there is no way to get any of the cars out."

While Lord Henry and Wilson conferred and went downstairs, James and I went to see Helena, who was sitting up in bed. Her room was filled with candlelight.

"Here," she said, giving me Lord Henry's watch. "Time the contractions."

James sat on the end of the bed looking frightened.

The contractions were coming about three minutes apart.

The house was creaking in the gale, thunder was crashing around, and inside, flashlights made patterns as footmen and maids ran to and fro.

James kept looking at Helena almost in a panic.

"James," she said between contractions, "don't worry. This is a perfectly natural process. I feel excited and ready to have this baby. After all, I have been preparing for it all these months. Women have been dropping babies since the beginning of people."

Lord Henry appeared. I gave him the results of my timing.

"Come along, Helena," he said. "We have things fixed up in the kitchen. I have the doctor on the phone. We trained for this, now we'll see it through together."

We helped Helena to the kitchen while James followed along behind.

A mattress had been placed on the big kitchen table. The room was full of candles. A pile of sheets and towels lay at hand. Cook was standing by. We helped Helena up on the table, and

Lord Henry examined her and then spoke on the phone to the doctor. The storm raged around us.

Helena looked around from where she was half sitting, propped up with pillows on the mattress. "You have done wonders," she said, and then panted and grimaced as another contraction more intense than the rest took her.

We waited and talked. Cook had prepared coffee in one of the pantries, which was lighted with more candles.

The contractions were now running about every minute.

"This baby is coming fast," she gasped. "Where are we going to put him?"

There was a moment of consternation. James, who was sitting on her shoulder occasionally licking her forehead, hopped off the table, beckoned to Johnson, who handed the light he was holding to me, picked up a candle and followed James into the dark house.

I wondered what James was about, but I knew he had explored every inch of the great hall, and sure enough, in about five minutes Johnson appeared carrying a baby basket from the old nursery on the top floor.

"There's a window broken in the nursery from a tree branch, but the rain is not coming in so I think it will wait till morning," he said. "James knew right where this basket was."

A small pillow and clean baby sheet from the layette, which was of course ready, prepared the basket for its new occupant.

Cook was now holding one of Helena's arms to give her something to push against while I held the other, and Lord Henry in a big, white apron monitored the baby's progress and talked to the doctor on the phone.

Not only were there no complications, Helena certainly was doing her part with enthusiasm.

Wilson had provided a battery-driven radio and we listened to weather reports from time to time. The storm, which had done considerable damage and closed most roads in the area, was to continue until about three in the morning and then abate. Power lines were down in many places and crews were already out trying to make repairs.

Lord Henry had concentrated the heavy-duty lanterns in the birth area. Candles flickered throughout the rest of the kitchen. Suddenly, the largest lantern began to flicker.

"Just what we need," he muttered as Helena let out a great gasp.

"James," he said, "you know the pantry near the entrance to the yard?" James nodded. "You can see in the dark; go and find the batteries that are kept there and bring me one, will you?"

James disappeared. In a few minutes he returned, dragging something behind him. It appeared to be some sort of rag wrapped around some large object.

"Clever fellow," said Lord Henry as Wilson undid the rag bag. In it were three batteries, which he promptly used to replace the dying ones. The light ceased to flicker.

James returned to Helena's shoulder and continued to lick her forehead.

In the end Lord Henry did not have to do much but catch the baby, once its head was free.

There he was, a baby boy, his head covered with pale fuzz, his tiny hands quivering. He let out a lusty gasping cry.

The doctor relayed instructions on severing the umbilical cord and delivering the afterbirth. Helena gasped and laughed, Lord Henry laughed and cried, and Cook wrapped the baby in a blanket and gave him to Helena to hold. The baby was screaming. Helena kissed him.

"Hello, Hal," she whispered. Then she gave him back to Cook, who put him in the basket on a nearby counter. James hopped on the counter and looked at the red, squalling baby. Very gently he touched the top of the fuzzy head with his furry cheek. The baby stopped screaming. James licked the little head very gently and began to purr. The baby breathed quietly, no longer frantic.

Suddenly, the lights went on. We realized the storm was no longer raging. Rain was still falling, but the wind was no longer blowing at gale force.

"Let's have lots of kids," said Helena.

Cook, who had had five children herself, gave Helena an affectionate hug and then took over the job of washing the baby and seeing to the mother while Lord Henry thanked the doctor and arranged that later in the day (it was now four in the morning), as soon as the roads were open, the doctor and a nurse would come to check on the patient. The nurse would stay as long as she was needed.

Lord Henry kissed his beloved wife. "We'll have as many as you want," he said, "but, I hope, not this way."

In due time, Helena, helped by Lord Henry and me, went back to her own bed with Henry George Ashton Steptson, who would in due time become the 25th earl of Haverstock, and James of St. James's, who would in due time become his godfather.

Wilson supervised the restoration of the kitchen, and everyone went to bed.

As we lay in bed James rubbed his face against my cheek and purred a happy purr. He began to lick me, but I knew it was not my face he was tasting but that of his future godson.

When we all woke up about noon, the storm had passed, leaving only ragged clouds and much cooler weather. I looked out my window to see the doctor and a nurse walking up the driveway. The main roads were now open, power had been restored, and in back I could hear the sound of a power saw cutting up the tree that had fallen in the yard across the garage doors.

I went down to breakfast, leaving James still asleep. I sat in the kitchen with Cook and Johnson, and we congratulated ourselves on how well we had come through the crisis.

I was drinking my second cup of coffee when Wilson appeared. He looked tired but his usual unruffled self.

"Lord Henry asked me to report that the doctor has pronounced both Lady Haverstock and young Hal to be in splendid shape," he said. "Nurse, who will stay for a week anyway, seems most pleasant, and I think we should be back in order by tomorrow. Weatherby and the outside staff are freeing up the garage at the moment."

"That's good news, Wilson," I said. "It was quite a night."

"Memorable," said Wilson. The phone rang. He answered it. "Miss Wettin," he announced. "Will you take it?"

"Certainly," I said. I greeted Fiona and told her the news.

"A proper heir! That's wonderful news indeed," said Fiona. "I think Etheria will have something to say! By the way, I guess you won't want to go to London this morning. You'll want to stay for a while."

"You can get to London?" I asked.

"Yes, the main roads are open, and my little house on the street had no problems, nothing fell on it."

"Would you take James and me up to London?" I asked.

"I should be pleased to take you, and if you can keep the cat quiet, I'll take him as well," she said in her sharp voice. "Be ready in an hour."

"Don't try the drive," I cautioned. "James and I will be waiting on the main road."

"Excellent," she said, and hung up.

So James and I said good-bye to a tired but happy Helena and Lord Henry and a sleeping Hal. The doctor had gone and Nurse Goodwin was now in charge of mother and baby.

Fiona had picked us up and deposited us at Baron's without incident. James slept on my lap all the way.

I spent the rest of the day getting my notes together, calling friends and contacts to say good-bye. James dozed on his table.

At five the guests began to arrive. Shep brought Jane and Anne. They were followed almost immediately by Peter Hightower, who sat in the big chair with James on his lap.

James insisted on being elegant and having his Lagavulin served in a glass instead of a saucer even though his whiskers kept getting in the way.

We cleaned out the larder and had some caviar, a dab of pâté and a lot of Stilton and Italian sausage.

I recounted the events of the night and described young Hal, without doubt the finest baby ever born. Peter promptly called Lord Henry to congratulate him and then settled back.

"Well, James," he said, as we were all warm and fed and relaxed. "You have had quite a time these past months." James purred happily. "Let's see, you captained a croquet team"— James stopped purring; that was a painful memory. "You directed a musical"—James grinned and waved a paw at Anne. "Exposed a fortune hunter and arranged a marriage—located two lost works of art and traveled some seven thousand miles to the other side of the world to do it."

James was now sitting up proudly on Peter's lap, acknowledging our applause. "Then you sponsored an unsuccessful cat food"—James snarled—"but you redeemed yourself and became a star witness for the prosecution of a felon and retrieved stolen property from an unsuspecting collector."

"Don't forget, he gave a benefit," said Shep. James hurled himself at Shep.

"And much more," mused Jane. "Think what he could do if he were properly managed."

In that instant James hopped from Shep's arms to mine.

I looked down at James. "She doesn't mean it, James. We all agree that, just the way you are, you're a fabulous feline."